Sathya Sai Baba

True Divine Parents for Humanity

Sathya Sai Baba

True Divine Parents for Humanity

A personal report

by

Gabriele Breucha & Anselm Keussen

Imprint

Bibliographical Information
of the German National Library:
The German National Library lists this
Publication in the German National Bibliography.
Detailed bibliographical data are available
on the Internet at
http://dnb.dnb.de

Authors: ***Gabriele Breucha & Anselm Keussen***

Production and publishing:
BoD - Books on Demand*, Norderstedt, Germany*
ISBN: 978-3-7562-7884-8
Available as paperback and e-book:
https://www.bod.de/buchshop

This is the newly edited and updated
English edition of the chapter:
Sri Sathya Sai Baba
of the original German book, pp 426-451:
Und was macht die Liebe?
ISBN: 978-3-00-044982-6

Imprint continued

*The **pictures** on the title and back cover are photos of a **poster of Sathya Sai Baba.***

*Pages 2 and 179 are photos of **Indian silk paintings,** which depict the Gods **Radha and Krishna,** who are a symbol for the Divine Mother and the Divine Father present in Sai Baba.*
The poster and the silk paintings were acquired by the authors in India in the 1980s and 1990s.

*The **pictures** on the pages: 3, 17, 68, 79, 97 and 117 are photos of posters, postcards and stickers acquired by the authors in India in the 1980s and 1990s.*

*The **picture** on page 151 is from the free Internet library **pixabay**.*

Om Sai Ram*

Introduction

Dears Readers,
cordial greetings. Still, you might ask:
'Sathya Sai Baba - who is that?!'

If you haven't switched on your mobile to research him in the first place.

Since Sai Baba has left his 'mortal coils' in 2011, there seems to be less public discussion on his personal life and his spiritual and worldly legacy.

What remains are the amazing social institutions - large ashrams, several local hospitals, schools, colleges, a big university, two world-standard maximum care clinics, huge water-providing projects - and countless selfless-service organisations all over India and the world, which have been founded by Sai Baba in such a solid way that they are all operating successfully even today, in 2022, about ten years later.
And there are almost endless amounts of books and media on Sathya Sai Baba and about the 'impossible' divine feats of his life.

A Matter of Balance

But there are also other reports, mainly in the internet, that decry Sai Baba's work, actions and intentions in very low ways.

Therefore, this book has now been written for spiritually interested people, who prefer to hear all sides out, who truly had contact from close quarters with this Avatar of Humanity - rather than jumping to spectacular, if below the belt conclusions, often long-distance, without ever seeing Sai Baba in person.

In order to help setting a hopefully more impartial - if thoroughly personal - perspective on these True Divine Parents of Humanity, as we have experienced Sathya Sai Baba, we have written the following essay.

It intends to integrate the various narrations on Sathya Sai Baba with our own exchange with him in such a way - so that you, Dear Readers, will hopefully be able to gain a better balanced imagination of this super-human being that often was simply called Sai.

All the best to you and your family

Gabriele Breucha & Anselm Keussen

* ***Om Sai Ram*** can be translated as:
Greetings to the primordial source of Love that is present in the Divine Mother and Father in you.

For Sai Baba
In deep Gratitude

And

Dedicated to
All people, families
And nations of this earth
Who are walking home
On the Godward path

Table of Contents

Sathya Sai Baba 3
Imprint 4
Introduction 6
In deep Gratitude 9
Table of Contents 10

True Divine Parents for Humanity 12
A first Glimpse 14
The Three Sais 18
Prashanti Nilayam live 20
Inner View - not Interview! 35
A Matter of Balance 40
Why fear, when I am here? 54
Some personal Experiences 64
Vegetable Dumplings 66
A very close Encounter 69
The Temple of Healing 72
Changing Colours 77
The Statue of Hanuman 80
Hidden Smoke 85
Metaphysics for the nuclear Physicist 89
Five Human Values 92
The Sarva Dharma Stupa 98
Sadhana 106
Just imagine 112
The inspiring Interview 118
A Letter and a Song 128
Saying goodbye to the Body 138

Table of Contents continued

Getting the Task done 142
Swami's Teachings through his Miracles.................... 144
A rare Transformation 145
Solace in a Name 146
Please let them live, Sir! 148
Spotless Devotion 152
Healing in the Jungle 156
The safe Instrument 159
Can you let me see it? 163

Epilogue 167
Timeless Time 170

The Authors 172
Websites on Sathya Sai Baba 175
Further Books by the Authors 175
Selected Bibliography 176
Advaita 178

Sathya Sai Baba
True Divine Parents for Humanity

*Family Life**

A young family is travelling to the ocean during summer vacation. Also on board is a small child, who comes to the sea for the first time with its parents.

Soon they are watching, as their toddler is setting out with his little sieve, shovel and bucket to create new worlds of sand and water at the shore.

Then the little kid has an idea - and it fills its colourful tiny bucket partly with the salty present of the slowly rolling waves.
All exited, the child carefully tip-toes back to its parents, so nothing is spilled. Then it proudly presents the small bucket to them, half-filled with salty water, only to proclaim rather seriously: 'Look - that's it!'

All the many people, who have written about Sai Baba probably felt a bit like this child, when they tried to fathom the infinite waters of the Sathya Sai Ocean!

Sathya Sai Baba has inspired countless writers and many media-makers from all around the globe to document the divine enigma of his resounding message, works and life in very detailed books, films and websites.

**Source see Bibliography.*

Therefore - we asked ourselves - which purpose would it serve to write 'yet another book' on the loving mystery that Sai Baba was and is?
Trying to 'describe' the eternally indescribable?

No, this is not our goal. Especially, as our memory of the reported events in Sai Baba's life may be incomplete in some cases. Also, we would have preferred to indicate the exact sources of our remembered quotes, which was not possible for time-related reasons.
But you can find them easily, because there are so many comprehensive reports, articles, books and media on Sathya Sai Baba already - and a selection that contains all the details of the events mentioned in this text can be found in the *Bibliography* at the end of this book.

In addition, our own lives, works and writings have been influenced and shaped by Sai Baba - or Swami, as he liked to be called - to such a degree that we feel it is appropriate to share a summary of our experiences with this God in human form - with all interested readers, but also with the readers of our other books, see page 175.

Books that would never have been written in this form without the benevolent and divine guidance and living example of Sathya Sai Baba.

A first Glimpse

'Sai Baba,' my friend said, 'this is Sathya Sai Baba of India, a great yogi and spiritual master - but are you really listening?' she asked me, as I had gotten so absorbed by the person on that postcard I had noticed next to the door.
Scrutinizing the cherub-like face above that orange robe and impressed by the huge Afro-Look the person in the picture was sporting, I answered cautiously:
'Well, one of those many Indian Gurus, as it seems - but there is something alive in his face . . . and what is he doing or teaching, this particular Baba?,' I asked back, while I still looked at the timeless face in front of me.

My friend paused for a while. Then she smiled and said:
'It's quite similar to the message of Christ - or to the core of all major religions - that we should love and serve each other, instead of harming others and clinging to worldly goods.
And that we should remember our own Inner Spark of the Divine', she added.
But then she continued, somewhat shyly at first:
'And Sai Baba is working many miracles every day - like curing the sick, or manifesting things . . .
'Red Alert!' my science-oriented medical mind called out, 'manifesting things' - in a nuclear reactor, or what?'

But I managed to maintain a neutral face when I replied:
'Sounds interesting - and how much is he charging to his followers?'

My friend giggled a little and stated: 'Nothing. He isn't taking any fees for himself. Only donations for social projects, like feeding the poor, re-building villages or constructing and running schools and hospitals.
And you pay a small amount for room and board, if you want to stay at one of his two Ashrams near Bangalore - today again Bengaluru - in South India.'

That was back in the beginning of the 1980s.
And step by step, my initial scepticism was changed into a questioning curiosity, when reports by a couple, who had personally seen Sai Baba in India, confirmed those informations.

Eventually, a friendly fate named Nancy arranged things in such a way that *Howard Murphet's* book:
Sai Baba - Man of Miracles claimed my full attention.

Written by a no-nonsense Australian - who had worked in the UK chemical industry in the PR-section before the war and had headed the British Military Press Corps that reported on the Nuremberg Nazi-Trials - this was a truly impressive book.

Evidently a book by a very clear-minded and rational person - but still: How could all those 'impossible' miracles be true, like 'creating' rings, necklaces, Swiss watches or airplane-tickets by the wave of his magic hand and from thin air?! And how did Sai Baba solve the problems of a celibate life?

Then, a quiet voice inside of me mentioned:
'And if only a fraction of Howard Murphet's book is true - it would always be enough to justify a journey to India, to see and experience for yourself, who this Sathya Sai Baba really is!'

In the end, the result was an expedition to India in 1985, including two inspiring 14-day stays at Sai Baba's Ashram Prashanti Nilayam, which I - Anselm - did by myself.

Later on, we - Gabriele and Anselm - were able to stay at Sai Baba's Ashrams during several visits to India.

Being deeply grateful to Sai Baba for his loving guidance in our lives, we were shocked to hear about some rather sinister accusations against him that circulated in the Internet since about the turn of the millennium.
During the years since 1985, we have been able to see and experience for ourselves that Sai Baba's divine personality was as genuine as his superhuman abilities.

And we have researched major parts of the available literature and other media on the 'Sai-Phenomenon' rather thoroughly - all of which only confirmed our confidence in his actions.

Despite this, we had to face strong doubts and difficult inner battles, when those rumours about transgressions or even abuse were first spread in the internet.

And it took quite a while, until we came to terms with those dark insinuations. How did that happen?
Well, mainly by looking at the 'whole picture' of Sai Baba's message, his works and his impact on the human society, next to our personal impressions from our visits to his main *Ashrams* in India.

The result of this sometimes tedious process has now been compiled in the following pages - in order to assist all interested readers in forming their own image and opinion of the True Divine Parents of Humanity, who Sathya Sai Baba was, is - and is going to be, as you yourself maybe will see.

The Three Sais

While the world was watching - first in small, later in ever increasing numbers of seekers - Sathya Sai Baba had shown himself to be 'Love in Action' ever since the tender age of fourteen years, when he first declared his Avatarhood.

On that day, Sathya Narayena Raju, which used to be his civil name, turned into Sathya Sai Baba, which means:
True Divine Mother and Father!

But Sai Baba isn't 'only two', meaning Mother and Father of Humanity, no - he is hopefully 'even three'!
How that?

Now, for one thing, there once was a holy man that used to be called Sai Baba of Shirdi, who evidently had also displayed very similar paranormal powers.
He had lived from - around - 1835 until 1918, and had devoted his whole life to helping others, sometimes also employing amazing *'leelas'* or 'miracles'.

While dwelling both in a somewhat dilapidated Mosque and in an old Hindu-Temple, he was working tirelessly to enable understanding, peace and further cooperation between the often fighting people of Islamic and Hindu faith.

As we will see below, Shirdi Sai Baba 'preceded' the later Sathya Sai Baba, who often stated that Shirdi Sai had been his previous incarnation.

And on top of all this, Sathya Sai Baba - 1926 to 2011 - has already predicted that he will even return for a third incarnation, as *Prema Sai Baba*, the Divine Mother and Father of Love, because Prema means Love in *Sanskrit*, the ancient Indian language.

In other words, *Sathya Sai Baba* himself has promised to be a 'Triple Avatar', to help humanity in coping with its mostly ego-made global crisis.

Hm. A *'Triple Avatar'* . . . interesting enough.
But what did it really look like, that 'Love in Action', which Sathya Sai Baba has shown throughout his life?

Prashanti Nilayam live

How did Sai Baba interact with his endless visitors from all the continents and nations of the earth?
How did he live?
And what remains of his work today?

Let's begin with the first question. Considering Sai Baba's global renown and his awesome paranormal abilities, he still was quite accessible - for Indians from any caste or creed, as well as for people from around the world.

'There is only one caste, the caste of humanity', Sai was often explaining.

Ancient sacred chants - *Omkar, Mantras* and *Bhajans* - accompanied by traditional holy dances called *Kirtanas* mark the beginning of the day in *Prashanti Nilayam*, the Abode of Peace Supreme, as Baba's ashram next to Puttaparthi is called. These chants and dances start as early as five o'clock in the morning.
And during Sai's life-time, one was well advised to be up that early, in order to 'sit in line' when tokens were drawn to decide, which of the lines was to go first into the temple precincts to see the *Avatar*.

These enchanting mornings, sitting 'online' on the sands of *Prashanti Nilayam* - with no internet at all, during the 1980s and 1990s - still remain etched forever in our memories.

Ladies and Gents each separate forming their lines quietly in the early morning cool under the coconut-trees, where the birds were wildly welcoming the new day, while the powerful Indian sun slowly rose to play with some first rays in the lush fans of the trees.

These special surroundings fit well with everybody's anticipation of soon seeing the Divine in human form directly.

Now both women and men walked in, line for line, and then settled in their respective quarters of the large temple-compound. In earlier years, until the late 1980s, the visitors were seated on fine sand.

When ever more people came to the *Ashram*, Sai Baba had a huge and beautifully decorated hall constructed right in front of his temple during the beginning of the 1990s, which is named *Sai Kulwant Hall,* so people were better protected from the sun.
Now we go back to witness the ongoing early morning procedures in *Prashanti Nilayam*.

As all had settled - and after a little while of timelessness - a gentle music would begin to play, swiftly focussing everybody's attention. Because this was the moment we all had been waiting for.
In the light of the new day, Sathya Sai Baba appeared from his quarters in the temple, his orange robe and his amazing halo of full black and curly hair clearly visible.

At the same time, the invisible impact of Sai Baba's powerful presence could be felt. Slowly, he would walk towards the women's side, sometimes 'writing in the air' with his right index finger - then again seemingly lifting up the air in a spiralling movement that he made with his whole right hand.

Just those apparently simple gestures have again and again cured 'incurable' diseases, brought back lost jobs, avoided accidents in a surprising way - or calmed the waves in fighting families.

But now *Swami*, as Sai Baba mostly liked to be called - which means Lord or Master - reaches the front lines of the women, most of them in colourful Indian *Saris*.

Vibhuti - a Ray of the Divine

Here and there, he briefly speaks with several of them or he accepts some letters. And then, it is happening:
With a few turns of his superhuman hand, he is now manifesting *Vibhuti,* as this sacred ash is called.
It should be remembered at this point, that Sathya Sai Baba 'produced' this holy ash probably dozens of times every day - to protect, to heal and to transform his followers on the spiritual path.

Depending on the situation, this blessed and freshly created ash could vary from light grey powder of Jasmine scent up to the darker, more solid compounds of medicinal smell, which are reported as well.

And Baba happily worked this 'small miracle' - from his own perspective - again and again, for those many ailing or doubting visitors - to cure, to convince and also to motivate.
Reports on those amazing powers of Sai Baba's glorious Vibhuti abound in media and literature - a diabetic condition or a drinking habit that was eliminated, cancers of various kinds that were cured, or this heart-, eye- or ear-operation, which became superfluous, after the healing sacred ash had been ingested.
Here a less spectacular, but still special anecdote that is connected with this amazing Vibhuti, told from memory.

Healing Vibhuti for whom?
A woman who had a number of problems in her life went to see Sai Baba. At the same time, she had a cat that had fallen sick, which she had left in a friend's care.
But by the time she reached the Ashram, she didn't think of her cat any more, as she was so preoccupied with all the health issues in her family and other problems.
Later, she was very grateful as Swami was talking with her. Knowing all her troubles, he gave her small parcels of Vibhuti for her afflicted family members and herself.
The woman was overwhelmed with joy.
Beaming happily - she thought she was to leave now.

But when she took a first tentative step, Sai called out to her and said: 'Wait, wait - this here is for your cat now!', while he handed her an additional packet of Vibhuti - for her sick cat she entirely had forgotten about!

With this, we're going back to the events of the morning *Darshan,* which signifies personally meeting and seeing a Divine person.
As we've been watching, Sai Baba gently floated along and through the women's lines, blessing, taking letters or at times writing a first OM with chalk on the slate of a first-year disciple. But he also had a very 'down-to-earth' humour.

When a woman repeated her ardent wish:
'Swami, I want a child from you!' a little too often during *Darshan,* he replied with a gentle, if impish smile:
'Well, right here and now?!' which solved and saved the situation in an unexpected way.

While Swami moved along and through the lines of the women like this, chatting, patting, taking letters, or making and giving Vibhuti to some, he now gradually approached the men's side, who were mostly dressed in white summer clothes.

And at rare occasions, he would take a step back from the lines or two - and then, only for some moments, his face mirrored all the messages he was receiving from the many thousands of devotees present - on the inner plane and virtually at the same time!
The variety and intensity of those countless bundled emotions appeared as one living flow on his face - but only very briefly - maybe to let us share his constant connection with all of us on this inner mental plane.

But in the next instant, he could be fully concentrated again, wandering towards that sea of white-clad spiritual aspirants on the men's side.

As he approached them, Sai Baba in his orange robe, who was of moderate frame himself, was joined by two 'body-guards' in white or in the Khakis of a Colonel - and they had quite an impressive physique.

Which at times even proved necessary, when whole flocks of those men - mostly Indian, but not only - quickly surged forward in their religious fervour, so close to the original source, intending to 'dive' at Baba's feet, so to speak.

But then these two protecting 'towers' at the side of the spiritual giant leapt into action, gently prodding those clusters and waves of emotional men away from his divine feet.
But soon, Sai Baba directed his path straight through the lines of these men again, which sometimes turned out to be a challenge for his two tall helpers, trying to keep up with him - to receive, for instance, a thick bundle of letters, which Sai had collected so far.

How to read letters
But what were those letters for? Well, these letters were one tangible form, by which Sai Baba's visitors were able to hand all their difficulties, trials and tribulations in written words to him.

Many can testify that Sai didn't really 'need' those informations in the envelopes given to him. Because on numerous occasions they could witness, as he had one of them pick any letter they decided to take - but only to give them the exact details of the letter, anonymously of course, which could later be verified on the spot as the letter was opened.

Letter refused, as it seems

One very special twist in this letter-interaction with Swami is revealed in the following episode.

An Indian couple got in touch with Sai, but only the woman had real faith in him, while her husband was a doubter.

At times he said: 'Well, to me it seems that this Sai Baba is only for the rich!' and didn't believe that he would take notice of him at all.

Now this couple had a daughter, who was to be married soon. According to Indian custom, her parents had found three possible young men, but hadn't decided yet, who was to be the groom.

Then the woman said to her husband: 'Why don't you write a letter to Swami, asking him about the three candidates and who is the right one?!'

Only partly convinced, this man did so, including the three names. But he still thought that Sai was 'only for the rich' when he closed the envelope to take it to *Dashan* at the next opportunity. Then he sat there and waited.

And was all aghast when Swami took his letter!
Seconds later, though, Sai threw that letter right back at this doubting person!

While catching the refused letter, the disappointed man thought: 'Oh well - I knew it before - he is only for the rich!'
And with similar words he brought the sealed envelope back to his wife right after the *Darshan* session.

She looked surprised for a moment - but then she said to him: 'Perhaps we should open the letter, so we can see what's inside?' she suggested.

He answered: 'Dear, I know what's inside, I put it there - but fine, let's have a look.' And on opening the letter, they found that two of the names had been crossed out - so only one candidate remained.

What didn't remain were the doubts and prejudices of the husband and father, who hadn't only found the fitting groom for his daughter, but also the ultimate spiritual home for his family and himself.

But which significance do those letters carry, one might ask, considering Baba knows the contents, not only of all these letters - but of any person's heart, mind and soul as well?!

So, Sai doesn't need these letters - he is informed of our situation and of our problems on the inner plane.

Still, and in addition to this 'instant knowledge', Sai Baba also read the letters given to him.

As it seems, the writing of those letters to Sai was more instrumental to us, his followers, in giving us the opportunity to concentrate on our questions and prayers to the Avatar.
While the morning was slowly getting brighter, Sai Baba moved among the men, exchanging some inspiring words with several of them - and occasionally allowing *Padnamaskar,* the touching of his divine feet.

What sounds strange to our 'western ears', is quite normal in India, even in worldly life, towards parents or teachers, for instance, where the touching of the feet denotes respect by honouring the elder or holy person in this way.

But this thing with the letters - does Sai Baba really 'know everything'? Actually, it might be helpful to find out the answer to this question in your own life, Dear Reader - but countless visitors of Sai Baba's ashrams can affirm that yes, he did, down to the smallest details of their life.
And not only what was close at hand - if one of his followers had a mother in Nairobi or so, who for instance had suffered a cardiac infarction, Sai would take him aside and tell him that his mother had to go to the hospital!

Shaken, but still sceptic, the devotee placed a long distance call to Africa to find out.

And when the mother had explained all about her heart-attack and surgery on the phone, she might have continued by telling her son in India that she had dreamt about a small man in an orange gown and Afro-Look, who had told her that she would get well now . . .

Back to that ever brighter morning in the ashram, with those hundreds to thousands of Sai devotees sitting on the ground, where Sai Baba had come out of his rooms to give morning *Darshan* to the assembled multitudes.

Beginning on the left, he had traversed the numerous and colourfully shining lines of the women, then he had wended his way through the men's side towards the right, where he by now had almost completed his morning walk amongst his devotees, followed by his tall helpers, who carried all the bundles of letters with those uncounted prayers to him.

Then, there is the gentlest stir in the collective field of the sizeable crowd, as Sai, the Divine Mother, and Baba, the Divine Father, present in this slender body clad in orange, is beginning to move his right hand, while he exchanges some seemingly casual remarks with a young Indian man who is sitting quite a few rows away from Swami on the floor.

By now, he is watching with his full attention - as does everybody else - how Baba proceeds to circle his magic hand a few times.
A timeless moment of creation later, he catches the just materialized object from mid-air - and then he holds it up for the young man and all of us to see. It is a simple, golden shining ring. For that young man!

And it is as heart-warming as it is heart-opening to see Sai Baba wading through the numerous lines of ecstatic men, who are trying to touch Swami's feet or to catch a glance of the freshly created ring.

But when Sai just looks at them - they all make way as if moved by huge unseen arms. Finally Sai Baba has reached far enough, so he can now hand the ring to the deeply moved youngster with outstretched arms.
Then he harbours this rare token of divine grace near his heart, to cover it from those many interested eyes.

And this incident during public *Darshan* was a very special one, because Sai Baba showed his divine powers only at seldom occasions in front of larger crowds.

By now, Sai Baba had completed morning *Darshan* and was about to walk back to the temple.
When he had gone inside, the whole congregation of many hundreds to thousands of Sai devotees began to sing *Bhajans* - Indian religious songs in praise of God with their specific lilting tunes.

These *Bhajans* went on for a good half-hour to an hour, which made the following silent meditation - under the palm trees or inside the temple - feel like a dive into a still and vitalizing pond.
But were those 'short interactions' during *Darshan* in the morning and afternoon the only way to communicate with this divine incarnation?
Before we move on to answer this question as well as we can, we should point out that 'only' seeing Sai Baba from afar during *Darshan* has had profoundly transforming and healing effects in many cases.

A serious Situation
For instance in a man of simple standing, who didn't really believe in Sai Baba, as he was also thinking that Baba was only a Guru for the rich.

But as he was afflicted with spreading 'incurable' cancer, he finally visited the Ashram, still deep in doubts.
And these doubts didn't relent, because he could only see Swami from afar, with no chance of talking about his predicament. Which went on for around two full weeks!
Then this man's allotted time in the Ashram was ending, as he had to leave - also to see his oncologist again.

Very disappointed that his lines at the men's side had never been up front, so he hadn't been able to hand his letter or even speak to Sai, this man left the Ashram full of his previous ideas that Sai Baba 'was only for the rich' and that Gurus weren't his thing anyway.

Having thus dismissed his stay at *Prashanti Nilayam* as of little avail, he returned home.

A while later he went to his doctor's clinic, to discuss the further treatment of his condition.

The doctor of oncology did some tests on him.

Then he looked him deep in the eye - which this patient didn't feel so good about - only to order special ultra sound and CT-scans, to assess the growth and exact location of the known tumours.

Only a couple of hours after the scans had been done, the patient got a call from his physician to come to his office at the clinic immediately.
Which the man did on the spot - only to find a somewhat dishevelled doctor, who congratulated him on the completely unrealistic fact that now all his tumours had vanished!

It took the patient a while to digest this unexpected turn of events for the better - but then he remembered his recent stay with 'the *Guru* for the rich' - and soon felt humbled by gratefulness.

Just this one case of many illustrates clearly that we should never underestimate the transforming field of Sai, be it like this, during *Darshan,* at a distance - or on the inner plane.

Sai Baba's Discourses

And now we return to our question from above, about other options to meet Sai Baba in addition to *Darshan* in the morning and in the afternoon.

Well, for one thing there were Baba's discourses, on major holidays, for instance - *Rama's* and also *Krishna's Birthday* as well as *Christmas* being some of them.

At such occasions, Sai would often be speaking to huge crowds of tens to hundreds of thousands of people.

But why did he call his speeches discourses, although just one person, Baba, seemed to be talking to us!?
This was a question that hadn't only bothered us for some time, but many others that were new to the Sai phenomenon as well.

And this lacking insight persisted in us, until we finally realized, as countless followers of Sai have done before us, that *Swami* is constantly aware both of our individual and collective mind.

Which means that he 'heard' all those thoughts or mental questions that were projected to him from the crowd on the inner plane.

That is one of the reasons, why Sai sometimes seemed to deviate from his line of thought in rather abrupt ways.

Hearing an urgent mental remark from one person in the assembly, he often answered it directly - and only when that had been accomplished, he returned to his previous message.

As we can see from these examples, contact with Sai Baba was - and is - quite independent from any specific outer environment, because these *Divine Parents of Humanity* did large parts of their healing work on the inner plane.

Vibhuti on pictures of Sai Baba in the Ashram in 2012.

Inner View - not Interview!

Despite those facts, well-known to all informed visitors of Sai's Ashrams, we all shared the common dream of being called for a more personal exchange with this incarnation of the Divine - the dream of being selected for an *interview,* as these meetings with Baba in small groups, as a couple or individually were called.
Often he advised us: 'Inner View - not Interview!' in order to remind us of the more important *inner contact* with our own divinity, with our own *inner Sai*.
Hearing this, we kept on practicing our meditations with a deeper dedication - but we still were dreaming of this one day, when all doubts and problems would be cleared and taken care of in the personal vicinity of the Avatar of the age, in that special grace named *interview!*

And there were many, who seemingly 'never got a chance' for this form of contact for decades - next to some quite fortunate others, who were invited often.
While on the other side of the globe, a person might cry out to Swami for help, without ever having seen him in person - and in many cases, Sai would hear the prayer and come to the rescue!
Interview - or Inner View? And how do you feel about it?
For the ever increasing stream of visitors to Sai Baba's main Ashrams in the 1990s, however, the choice was mostly 'inner view', as the occasions for an interview seemed very few now, in the face of the multiplying multitudes that prayed for one every day.

By the time of the turn of the millennium, we had given up all those unrealistic hopes towards a more personal meeting with Swami.
But we were very grateful to be so near to him again, in *Prashanti Nilayam,* the home of peace supreme, where we could see him daily - sometimes from close quarters - during morning and afternoon *Darshan.*
In addition, we enjoyed singing *Bhajans*, sometimes even within the temple. And then, when all the songs had ended, sitting in quiet meditation.
Besides, there were lectures on spiritual themes and other group activities, in which Sai devotees met that originated from the same home country.

And in the 1990s, we had always found at least one German speaking group that would meet on a regular basis during the pauses of the Ashram time-table.
Between ten and twenty Sai devotees from various parts of Germany gathered in the afternoon in the shade of some of the big Ashram trees at those occasions.
There, we all joyfully sang *Bhajans* and a variety of other religious songs.
Then we meditated together in Swami's timelessness.
Very rarely, a member or two of the group had been called for an interview by Sai Baba, so they were able to share some of their impressions at one of the next group meetings.
A theme that remained from those reports was this:
'He really knows - nay, is everything!
Even our innermost thoughts are open to him!'

But when we returned to Baba's *Ashram* in October 2000, no German group was to be found. And by that time, Swami was only seeing well organized groups that carried the colours of their home country.
And that meant: No group, no chance for an interview with the *Avatar* - not even the slightest chance!
Rather bleak perspectives.

How it still happened that a small German group was 'manifested' at the last moment - Sai Baba is often and rightfully called the 'Last Minute Guru' - and how this ephemeral group then, on this cold and rainy October morning was called against all odds - but no, now we're really moving way too far ahead!

Before we continue with the events of this drizzly and seemingly thoroughly unpromising morning just some chapters further, towards the end of this book, we now would like to return to the second of the questions we had asked in the beginning of this book.
The first one had been about Swami's personal exchange with people on a larger scale, which we have tried to sketch in the above text.

And now you may remember that the second question was about Sai Baba's legacy - in India and around the globe.
Or in other words: What remains of Swami's message, his mission and his work today, about ten years later - in the 2020s - and what does that signify for our future?

All the impressive works of his life are a living testimony for this mission.

Schools for girls and boys, secondary schools, a multi-campus university with top performance, several local hospitals - and two huge clinics with the maximum international level of care - including heart and kidney operations - which are by now, in 2022, covering all major specialties in medicine.

In this diversity of Indian and International kinder-gartens, preschools and schools, all pupils were and are taught according to the *Educare-Principles*, which don't only train memory by filling in 'knowledge', but also further the development of the five *Human Values* in those children and youngsters.

Then there are assistance projects through *Seva*, a form of selfless service, which is for instance employed in case of catastrophes, floods or earthquakes . . . but also in poor villages and city-neighbourhoods.

For which purpose tens and hundreds of thousands of pupils, students and other *Sai-Devotees*, or disciples of Sai voluntarily sacrifice their free time and engage their personal strength.

Even today, in 2022, about ten years after Sai Baba's transit on Easter Sunday 2011, these 'Seva-operations' are carried out regularly, facing the COVID pandemia.

And we find a *Pure Water Project* for all in all more than ten million people! Including the metropolis of Chennai, formerly called Madras.
Just Sai Baba's material heritage - which certainly is not the most important aspect - is estimated at between two and seven billion dollars, which is mostly invested in the above mentioned *Social Activities* - or designed to ensure their future maintenance.

And this entire range of activities - the various schools, hospitals, *Seva* and Water Projects, plus the colleges and university - they have one thing in common:
They all are completely free of any fees!
Everything was and is financed and kept going by the donations that were and still are given voluntarily to the trusts that were established by Sathya Sai Baba. - And by the dedicated and loving work of countless Sai devotees.

By the many followers and helpers of Sai Baba, who are the members of the *Global Sai Family*.

But before we continue to further illustrate who and how *Sathya Sai Baba* was - and is - by quoting some examples, we would like to comment on some of the unfriendly allegations that have been made against Sai Baba - especially on the internet - for many years.

In this, we will try to understand why Sai Baba acted as he did in that context - and which meaning it still might carry today.

A Matter of Balance

Some authors had wanted to write about Sai Baba - very impressed by his 'miracles', his tireless commitment to social projects of all kinds and by the personality change to the positive in most of the people who visited him. -
But several have reported the following reaction from Sai Baba, when they asked him if he would agree, if they were to write a book about him:
'My dear one, you are enthusiastic about those so-called miracles - which, however, only somewhat resemble my 'visiting cards'. -
And you are impressed by my other work as well.

But you should also be aware of the fact that some very unpleasant rumours are circulating about me.
Therefore listen to all sides, enquire about the rumours - and, most important, observe my personal way of life carefully, because:
My life is my message!

Before we go on to investigate other, indeed wonderful and loving aspects of Sai Baba, we would like to follow his own advice here as well, which includes commenting on these - often very lopsided - 'accusations' against Sai Baba as best we can.
To begin, we would like to remind you, Dear Reader, that almost all prophets or God-like persons, who have appeared in the history of humanity - were invariably fought vehemently - often even to the point of blood!

Be it on the grounds that those spiritual pioneers were supposed to be 'damaging to the state', would 'contribute to the decline of good morals' or - especially popular again and again - that they were 'blaspheming the Gods'!

Here, we may also think of the deeply meditative and all empathetic *Buddha*, for example, who was mortally poisoned anyhow.

Further of *Socrates*, the clear-sighted, wise mastermind and ancestor of most western philosophical systems that had emanated from *ancient Greece*.

Then there is *Moses,* the founder of the Jewish religious community, who then had been expelled from home, murdered and persecuted, first by Egypt, then by Babylon and finally by almost all narrow-minded countries and people of the world, for centuries and millennia - up to the unspeakable Holocaust of them in Germany's historical error of the Third Reich.

Then, of course, we think of *Jesus of Nazareth*, who, as a social revolutionary and alleged King of the Jews - in the sense of a secretly planned coup d'état - was condemned to death on the cross by the power obsessed temple priests and by the provincial governor of the Roman Empire.
But already Christ needed a 'traitor' to complete his mission, as paradox as this may seem.

And we remember the way in which the first small cells of a later world religion - that had been founded by this Aramaic 'miracle rabbi' and Preacher of the commandment of love - were persecuted as a 'sect', while their members were tortured and killed indiscriminately.

Here the irony of history formulated as a question:
What would the socially engaged, tolerance and love preaching Aramaic-Jewish miracle worker and healer, who also had proclaimed those important *Human Values* in the *Sermon on the Mount* - what would he think about all the many different Christian Churches of today and around the globe?

The answers are easy to find in the Bible, if we remember the actions of *Jesus Immanuel the Christ* towards the often dogmatic and self-righteous religious and state institutions and their 'representatives' in his historical time.

Admittedly, this is only one specific perspective - if an important one - upon the Christian Churches and especially the 'Family of Christianity' of today.
And we, the authors of these lines, belong to that family.

But today's helpful *Caritas*, or Charity, which is the greatest strength of the churches, must not hide the many difficulties in the sometimes obsolete 'system' and constructions of 'The Church of Today'!

This goes for the role of women, the attitude towards gay priests; then money-laundering - and the uncounted sexual assaults in churches and schools . . .
Swift evolution and reform is necessary here.
Right now and in the spirit of love.

But let's return to the widespread patterns of violence, degradation and persecution towards the great religious founders and reformers.
Even *Mohammed the Prophet* - who had initiated the great religious community of the Muslims - first had to struggle with pronounced inner doubts himself.
According to the scripture, he had a series of powerful and disturbing visions of the glorious Divinity, mediated by the *Archangel Gabriel,* while he had retreated into the solitude of a cave in the desert. But his wise wife, *Chadidsha,* helped him to clear those troubling doubts.

Later, after he had formulated and proclaimed the main features of the present *Qur'an,* he had to defend himself against the fierce attack of a far superior military force, which had been sent to field against him by the old caste of priests in *Mecca* - and by their allied state rulers, who were in power at that time.
Despite this huge disadvantage, *Mohammed's* inspired warriors were able to achieve a surprise victory against the seemingly overwhelming multitude of enemies.
In this context, the current, sometimes difficult position of women in several - not all! - Islamic countries is a bit surprising in terms of developmental history.

Because this special tradition goes back to a *Holy Man* and *Prophet,* who was one of the few married founders of a religion - and who gradually strengthened the rights of women in his time.

And at the beginning of his visions, he even was strongly encouraged in this by his former employer and later wife - *Chadidsha* - to make his teachings public.
In the hour of his deepest inner doubts, whether all the messages he had received were really genuine.

Lao Tzu, Confucius, Zoroaster, Luther, Padre Pio, Gandhi, and the *Dalai Lama* - what elucidates from the often so harsh fate of these social and religious transformers and founders?

In many cases, this development almost regularly seems to follow a specific historical pattern.

On one side, we frequently find a very rigid religious and governmental structure of coercion, which has been in place for a long time already, and that is dominated by the wishes for power and possessions that mostly emanate from the old Angst-controlled ego-spirit of the ruling class.

This is often quite heavy a burden for the 'people in the street', which often takes on absurd dimensions of overly dogmatic 'nannying', together with material exploitation in way too many cases.

Then, as a counter-balance and new movement at this impasse, there appears a charismatic, mostly social-reformist person, who is often radiating a strong aura of truthfulness and justice - and even has healing powers to cure the sick in some instances.
That person is mostly peaceful and authentic - and has a genuine ability to love all, which is experienced directly by her or his followers.
In some special cases, she or he commands enormous abilities that go far beyond any human possibilities of the time - and are therefore perceived as inexplicable divine miracles by the others.

Because of these qualities, this person is gradually gaining an increasing number of adepts, followers or disciples - but they soon begin to be a thorn in the side of the aforementioned and way too often rigidly power-hungry 'authorities'.
Especially, since the new and prophetic God-like leader, who is mostly preaching non-violence, social justice and charity, is by now pointing ever more urgently at the real problems of that society, which are usually caused by a massively exaggerated spirit of possessiveness, fear and ego in the leading classes.

Now the strong influx of followers which these radiant *Incarnations of Love* often find - if we want to understand them this way - induces, of course, even more fears in the religious and state 'leaders' than they had had already anyway.

Therefore these rulers resort to ever lower means and methods to intimidate or eliminate the *New Message of Love*, especially by getting hold of its leaders. -

And over centuries and millennia even violence, torture, and murder have been 'found to be proper means', as we have seen above. Since 'the end allegedly justifies such horrible means' - if one wants to go along with such a questionable attitude.

Often, however, it is precisely this form of counter-pressure and counter-violence by the mostly ailing and outdated established 'powers' or traditional institutions, which really awakens and further fuels the liveliness of just those New Messages of Love.

A similar form of 'resistance' - especially from various religious institutions that seem to possess a 'dogmatic tenure of the truth' - has happened to the Oversoul, the phenomenon and the person Sai Baba.

Even an attempt on his life was made in the 1990s, in which two close helpers of his died.

As we will continue to summarize Sai Baba's message and work further below, for the moment only so much:
Like the prophets, reformers and God-men mentioned before, Sai Baba represents an approach of self-enquiry or *Sadhana* - primarily in Meditation, but also in all our thoughts, words and deeds. -

This is done to recognize and feel where we are rigidly and overly attached - often even holding on to obsolete behavioural patterns that are damaging to others or ourselves.
If we succeed in these, often rather painful insights - as they are frequently connected with deep and early injuries and fears - we may also learn to 'loosen up' our greedy and compensating ego-spirit step by step.

Like this, Sai Baba's message and actions are guiding us to the forever old and forever new way that is called 'Philosophia Perennis', the eternal ethical and religious stance in life - as we could translate that - which is the philosophy of love for our neighbour and for ourselves.
And the further we can follow this path, the more clearly we may recognize the divine nature of love in all we encounter - in the so-called others and within ourselves.

Everything that Sai Baba said, did and built - be it by way of his 'miracles', through his many *Educare* educational systems from preschool and elementary school to secondary schools and colleges, up to a university in India - and also worldwide; then by his impressive hospital projects *free of charge for patients*, or by way of his personal interaction with uncounted individuals, couples, families and - sometimes very large - groups:

And all these activities had one purpose only - they served to help us develop along the path of this
Eternal Philosophy of Love.

But don't we know that 'Good News' already?

Of course, exactly this form of personal development and attitude of cooperation basically characterizes the core of all known religions, such as the commandment to love each other, as we find it in the Mosaic religion, in Islam and in Christianity.

But Sai Baba explicitly *did not* want to found a new religion, as he has affirmed often enough.

Much rather, he advised all of us to remain with our own respective religion. At the same time, he admonished us, however, to practice it better and from our heart.

All this sounds very simple and good; so where is the problem?

It was Sai Baba's infinitely powerful and dynamic love-principle, which seemed to upset many people - very similar to Jesus Christ in his time. -

These people felt disturbed in their habitual, often narrowly woven life patterns, which then made them project their own and sometimes extremely malicious aggressions onto the *'Avatar'*, the Divine Incarnation of Love in a personal being of our time.

What are the main accusations in this context?

1.) Sai Baba's miracles supposedly were not real, but, as in the case of Houdini, Siegfried and Roy or David Copperfield, merely deceptive tricks, which Sai Baba allegedly wanted to use to win 'gullible believers' as followers, in order to 'glean money from their pockets'.

2.) Sai Baba was said by some people to be only a 'Guru for the rich', from whom he wanted gains for himself, again in terms of power and money.

3.) Probably the most serious accusation:
Certain individuals claimed that 'something was wrong' with Sai Baba's sexuality - and that he were abusing the pupils and students of his educational institutions.

In short, he was 'painted' in some media to be a harmful paedophile!

Since this last accusation goes the farthest, we will start with it.
First of all, it is quite undisputed that Sai Baba, as far as his physical aspect was concerned, has been displaying gay inclinations since his later youth.
On closer reading of the literature about Sai Baba, which meanwhile comprises hundreds, maybe even thousands of books worldwide, we find many, if mostly indirect references to Sai Baba's homoerotic side.

Some rather clear passages pertaining to this can be found in Prof. Kasturi's *Loving God.*

The most important questions: Why?, or even more central: 'What for?' did a godlike or even entirely divine being come to earth, in exactly this specific Indian as well as global temporal context, and equipped with a homosexually disposed body, will be discussed in further detail in a few moments.

But as far as the accusation is concerned that Sai Baba would have sexually abused young adolescents or even children - here are five facts we at least should take into account, when we are trying to find a balanced opinion or fair judgment in this regard:

1.) As we've mentioned in the beginning of this chapter already, Sai Baba has frequently and in public pointed out those low rumours that were circulating about him - and he even instructed people, who wanted to write articles or books about him, *to investigate* just these very rumours and accusations in detail.
Which secretly sexually abusive person would do this?

2.) As we have mentioned, Sai Baba lived his gay aspect rather openly, also in relationships with younger men.
And virtually all the young men who visited his Ashram knew about this - and many hoped for closer contact with him.
The internet campaign against Sai Baba in this matter contained the information that he deliberately had given one of his raw silk *Dhoti*s - a tied cloth that serves as underwear to the Indian - to some of his younger friends.

As a present - but no, not for themselves - much rather for the parents of those young gents!

Which teacher or priest, who actually is assaulting boys, would draw such an attention to that situation?

And again: Why? - and What for? did Sai Baba create this sharp focus on that specific topic? That still needs to be understood in more detail in the following pages.

3.) Sai Baba's whole message and his life's entire work are based on these principles:

Love all, serve all!

Ceiling on desires!

Help ever, hurt never!

Whoever is informed but slightly about the way in which Sai has carried out and built up this work for 85 years - and since age 14 in selfless and loving service to humanity, day in and day out, and has observed Baba's work from close quarters - a multitude of media are now available for this purpose, too - will at least consider it extremely unlikely that such a being would harm anyone - much less the children of his own schools, to whom he assigned the greatest value.

And this improbability increases further because - as we could often see with our own eyes - there always were an astonishing and quite public number of younger gents, also in small groups - from India and from around the world - who were waiting quite visibly for contact and closeness with Sai Baba.

And that in total freedom and fully self-determined! -
And so numerous at the same time, that Sai Baba could never have invited all of them.
And why? Well, there simply were way too many!

And some, often quite ambivalent people, who wanted that nearness - but were not invited - or not invited any more - went on to scatter those miserable rumours - mostly born of their personal envy and jealousy that was fuelled by their own unlived love.

4.) Sai Baba's paranormal abilities and how he used them is also a theme of interest in this discussion.

All the visitors to *Prashanti Nilayam*, who have observed and experienced Sathya Sai Baba for a longer time, are quite familiar with his 'miracle phenomena', which he only described as his calling card.

Confirmed by uncounted witnesses, Sai Baba has been re-defining the 'laws of nature', as they were known to us before - and that many times a day!

But when he performed his seemingly 'impossible' feats, he was always aiming at the learning effect in the hearts of his followers.

Away from greed, fear, hatred and violence - and instead, towards selfless service in serenity, trust and love.

Why fear, when I am here?

'Why fear, when I am here?' Sai Baba often used to say - sometimes difficult to understand for us 'Westerners' - because such claims could perhaps be made by a historical person, maybe 2000 years ago - but today?

Seems clearly mega-out! Or is it?

Well, Swami, as his devotees are calling him, was the one to do this for us 'modern people', when he for instance said the above sentence:
'Why fear, when I am here?!'
to his entourage in a seemingly awkward situation. -
For example, when the car he was going by - yes, he also used cars for transport - had run out of gasoline.

Insight by lacking Petrol
Which happened - perhaps intentionally at times, in order to experience a 'miracle' - at quite a number of occasions, as is well documented in the literature.

Then Baba, as he was also called, had a larger vessel or canister brought to him, which, depending on the situation, sometimes was filled with water.

Now Sai simply held his hand over the vessel - or he was stirring the water with a wooden stick - and presto! - the water turned into normal petrol that could be poured into the car's tank!

But when there was no water - this was no problem either! - Even entirely empty containers were filled by Sai Baba with a touch of his divine hand.

And the fullness of his powers was by no means limited to gasoline, as we will see further below.

But also Sai's other paranormal abilities - such as telekinesis, teleportation or telepathy, which are a remote movement or remote transport of an object, or the 'remote reading of someone's mind', respectively - are well documented many thousands of times.

Also, he could let completely forgotten memories come alive in real time for any visitor - and probably wouldn't have had any problem at all - if he had wanted to - to manipulate or delete the memories of his friends.
But this did not happen! Instead, some of them got *Dhotis* from him - for their parents!

5.) Conclusion:
Sai Baba wanted these 'accusations' against himself!
With his evidently unlimited abilities to change reality with his cybernetic options, Sai Baba could easily have prevented the media and internet 'scandal' about his gay aspect. -
Still, he clearly wanted - at which personal price? -
exactly this echo in the media!
But for what purpose?

In all this we should remember well that Sai Baba was pointing at an obsolete and erroneous colonial law.
And at obsolete and erroneous international laws.
All his life and by his own silent but well visible example.

Any further ideas?
Well, maybe also to direct full attention, in India as well as worldwide, towards the abusive and transgressive behaviour with many children and youngsters - in their families of origin, but also in schools, churches and other 'institutions'. -

So we can finally change the endless suffering that is caused by such damaging actions.
The pupils and students at Sai Baba's schools, colleges and university are 'the heart piece' of his work, as he himself has emphasized again and again.
He encouraged all of them, whom he saw as the future of India, to be the best they could in their life. -

To harm them - or any human person or being - just was not Sai Baba's nature - as far as we can say, according to our own experiences.

On top of all that, there has never been any substantial lawsuit against Sai Baba - and his schools, colleges and university always had and still have waiting lists - which parents would act like this - if these rumours were more than just rumours?

In other words, they were slander, which, as we have seen, was present against almost all of the holy religious founders and other sacred people.
Even the endlessly Rome-faithful *Padre Pio* was accused of 'improper behaviour' with nuns!

Which probably never happened - but if so, would that, mutual consent given, be such a horrible thing?!

Now that we have tried to somewhat understand the quality of Sai Baba's actions in the context of those rumours as well as we could, we'd like to return to the central question mentioned before.
Which goes, why did the *'Avatar of our Age'* choose to appear in a homosexually disposed body amongst us?

In order to understand this, we should begin with a first and tentative look at the role of homosexuality in India today.
Here, the vast majority of marriages are still 'arranged' by the parents of the bridal couple - as has been the case for many millennia.
And any sexual contact between women and men is usually taboo before marriage. This explains the 'detour into homosexuality' by some Indian men in the sense of a compromise solution.

If we walk down a typical Indian street, we often see young, but also older men who are holding hands.
But are they all gay? Maybe some.

Generally, the handling of physical contact between men seems to be more relaxed and playful in India than in the western world.
And in some of the Arabian countries there might also be comparable developments.

Now we must caution us at the same time to realize that this 'homosexual scenario' - also caused by the so far prevalent separation of the genders in Indian society - frequently seems to have the character of a silent area in Indian media, consciousness and conversations.

On one hand, 'erotic male friendships' are tolerated and accepted, even within official institutions, as a matter of fact and necessary - but on the other hand, also in the sense of a taboo, there is apparently only little or no talk about it.

And it is just this multiple 'tabooing' of all things sexual that often causes the danger that children are sexually abused, which is happening daily and way too often - everywhere in the world!

Is this situation really so surprising?

If we only look at our own historical development of the last one or two hundred years in Europe and the USA - probably not at all!

To refer to a well-known example in this context:

Even *Thomas Mann* - author of the *'Buddenbrooks',* then *'The Magic Mountain', 'Doctor Faustus'* and *'Joseph and his Brothers',* to mention only a few of his sublime works, which are definitely worth reading and carried by a spirit of great goodness - even he still had to hide his gay sexual inclinations, since they were not only socially denied but also punishable by law in his time!

And this has remained so - until the dreaded paragraphs of the penal code were finally deleted in many countries.

This 'separation from his ingrained nature' has often been a heavy burden for the 1926 Nobel Prize winner *Thomas Mann* and his family. -

But it is also true that this self-imposed 'denial' in part had the function of an inspiring 'driving force' or 'engine' for Thomas Mann as a writer, when he was creating the impressive works of his lifetime.

Today, at least in many countries, things have relaxed a lot in this respect.
Also India finally legalized gay love in 2018.

Now, there is the 'Love Parade', 'Christopher Street Day' and homosexual marriages and politicians are part of everyday life in many countries, to give some examples.

But there still are some 'comedians' who are not shy of 'bravely' aiming below the belt in such cases.

And where would the global LGBT-community be today without Sai Baba's courageous and self-chosen path?

Unfortunately, there are still way too many countries, where any 'gay life' is denied and suppressed - or even subject to capital punishment!
In *Ancient Greece*, however, they had - as far as this way of life is concerned - quite different customs and mores.
There, close friendships between young men and their teachers were a reality and considered entirely normal at that time.
Now that we've briefly reviewed those issues in our own recent history, we would like to go back to the original question about Sai Baba's gay life and its meaning on one hand; and, on the other, on the possible significance of the fact that he actively 'promoted' these rumours of abuse against himself.

The following are pure and very personal hypotheses, of course, and each and every one of us has to form her or his own opinion about this in the end, but it seems that we can roughly recognize the following elements.

1.) Sai Baba never tired of emphasizing:
'My Life is my message!'
If we take him by the word in this, then what might the example of his life be telling us?

Amongst other things, which we'll see below, his life seems to say:

'Live your physical nature, your erotic side and sexuality - also and especially, if you happen to be gay!

The aspect of anal sexuality, which is also called Yin-Yang Intimacy or Diamond-Ring-Union, belongs to our normal human nature; therefore you better re-integrate them into your love-live and enjoy them, if you want that.
But please treat each other with love and care, when you embark on this strong and sacred power!'

2.) Further his life might say to us:
'When I intensify these absurd rumours that some are circulating about me, I make sure that your attention is all focused on the issue of sexual child abuse - both in India and worldwide! Because this form of abuse results in serious and often lifelong damage for all involved.

Wake up from your 'suppressive trance' and also from your 'repressive taboos', concerning child abuse - mainly by living your own sexuality in a healthy way - and kindly amongst grown-ups!
And: 'I do not hesitate - despite all my abilities and despite my loving nature - to employ my popularity to sensitize you against those dark machinations - even if these false rumours depict me in a completely distorted way!'
At this point, it is good to remember that Sai Baba himself has predicted the huge storm in the media, which would drive many devotees away from him - for instance at his 60th birthday in 1985!

And how about the revelations of transgressions and abuse - including schools and churches! - in the western world?
Perhaps they also have to do with the attention, which Sai Baba directed on purpose towards this special focus?

3.) The main impulse, however, to the women and men of this world regarding human intimacy that is inspired by Sai Baba's courageous example -
'My Life is my message!' - certainly seems to be:
Cast off your obsolete shyness towards your anal, Yin-Yang or Diamond-Ring-Intimacy - and dare to be erotic, sexual and loving beings - also and especially amongst men!

Further, dare to live your *Anima*, your female aspect - no matter, if 'gay' or 'hetero', woman or man - Yin-Yang-intimacy harbours beautiful surprises, if you apply the loving patience to find them.

Sai Baba has set an example - of Living Love in all areas of human life - are we ready to follow this example?!
Do we still dare to dream?

Whether this very tentative interpretation of some of Sai Baba's actions is correct, is not for us to know.
But we had the occasion to observe him 28 years in person in India and in the media - and these seem to be the logical conclusions, as we have explained them above.

This indirect invitation to love, including gay love, also appears like a timely counterbalance to our collective patriarchal pre-psychosis of a new militant arms-race around the globe.

Therefore, the strict displacement of *anima*, *anus* and a*mor* that is prevalent in overly paternal societies, is evened out by a healing movement that ends this suppression - and integrates love instead - including gay love and Ying-Yang-Erotic.

To make sure that all - voluntary, self-determined and non-violent - varieties of loving union, be it on the physical, mental or spiritual level, are found by us.
Because these various forms of love are quite important for the development of our soul!

So much - or so little - about the homo-erotic aspect in Sathya Sai Baba - an issue, which obviously was so important for the *Avatar* or *Parentar* of our age - the divine father or parent-person of humanity - that he personally chose to live this variety of love.

Maybe in order to show us the way to peace and love between men - which then in turn serves our path to cooperation and unity in the human family. -
Just as Sai Baba's whole life has been loving service to humanity.

Some personal Experiences

In the beginning, Anselm had met Sai Baba personally in India in 1985. Later on, Gabriele and Anselm have been to Prashanti Nilayam together eight times from 1992 to 2011 - mostly also living in the *Ashram* or monastery that Sai Baba had built for his visiting devotees.

During all of these journeys to the *'Ultimate Experience'** Sai Baba was still alive - and we are deeply grateful for those journeys to him and for the encounters with him.
*This is the title of a book by *Phyllis Krystal*, the well-known American therapist and spiritual master, who also wrote: *'Cutting the Ties that bind'*. A cordial Thank you!

And we experience it as a divine blessing that we also were allowed to be with him in the year 2000 with a small German group and several Indians for a personal conversation called interview, to which we will return at the end of this book.
With these details about our journeys to and our life with Sai Baba we only intend to document that we have investigated and explored Sai Baba's phenomenon since 1984 until 2011 as well as we could.
Now you might ask: What do we perceive as the result of this long-term endeavour?

Sai Baba was and is an endless source of superhuman, unconditional and divine love, which he passed on generously and in an exemplary way to everyone who wanted his support.

And he never 'needed' anything from anyone! -
Much rather, time, space and matter were like plasticine for Sai, in his constant service to humanity.

And what about those who did not really 'believe' in the help, healing and miracles from Sai Baba? Often enough, they received them despite their doubts. And there are many staunch atheists, who gave their position a second thought, when Sai Baba had first materialized Vibhuti - healing ash - or other sacred objects for them - and then told them about central, game-changing or painful experiences in their lives down to the smallest detail.

Only to continue by discussing the current questions and problems in their work, family life and health situation with them. -
And all of this in a way, as if he had been there himself in each of these instances!

Even very hard-boiled 'rationalists', 'positivists' and even 'nihilists' arrived at an entirely new inner attitude that special way.

And it is this divine transformation of the heart within millions or billions of people, which is the true miracle and legacy of Sri Sathya Sai Baba of India!

Now a few more additional episodes from Sai Baba's life. Further details can be found in the *Bibliography*.

Vegetable Dumplings

To give a concrete example, we remember a report from Sai Baba's 'earlier years', about 1950-70s.
It is from: *Ganapati, Ra: 'Baba: Sathya Sai'* tome I & II.
The story went approximately as follows:
In his youth, Sai Baba often liked to travel overland with a group of people - mostly to visit and inspire several cities during the tour.

Sai loved the lush outdoors of India's nature and therefore often ordered the cars to be stopped for a picnic or dinner in the open air. -

Then he often chose the 'camp site' for picnic or meal himself, while he usually discovered the best places that even the most experienced 'local guides' had not known so far.
On such an outing, there once was a *driver* who did not like Sai Baba very much and had lots of doubts about him.
'This small person of just over five feet in that orange caftan with this odd 'afro-look' is supposed to be a God person or even God altogether?
Never in life! And he is also going by car and eats and talks like us! That can be no God!'

Then, in the evening, when food for dinner is distributed, the driver is standing near to Baba's place.
Now Baba is saying casually:

'Would you perhaps like some of those dumplings, filled with vegetables and baked in boiling oil?'

Although that kind of food mentioned by Swami was not even on the menu - these seemingly confused words of Sai still reached the doubting driver.

First, he looked into the void for a while - as if he were in shock. Next, he dropped everything from his hands - and then threw himself at Sai Baba's feet!

What had happened? A long time ago, the driver had been in the kitchen with his mother when he was a small toddler.
And she had prepared exactly those tasty vegetable dumplings in boiling oil, which Swami had mentioned.

Childishly ignorant, he had pushed the pot with hot oil from the stove - and he had burned himself violently while doing this.

He still had scars under his shirt from that accident.

When Sai had indirectly addressed this early episode of his life with his question, which he himself had forgotten long since - the man knew that Swami 'was for real' - and he immediately was in a good mood and very grateful to have found divine love in person.

Still, you have difficulties to believe that?! No problem.

Because knowledge - so they say - is power.
But not-knowing doesn't bother anybody either -
except we perhaps wait a little longer for the Light . . .

And therefore now a good example of Sai Baba's work, which is easier to check, because there is a building that bears testimony for this.

The Sri Sathya Sai Super Specialty Hospital and Heart Clinic near Prashanti Nilayam. Picture of th main buildings.

But let's go step by step.

A very close Encounter

This report is about a well-known British business man named *Isaac Tigrett*.
As a young man, he had wanted to create a nice surprise for his mother - and therefore had ordered a major US 'motor-cruiser' by ship to be brought to the UK.

When he went to the dock to pick it up, a wealthy man greeted him, who offered him about three times the US price for the car.

Tigrett sold it. - He had discovered a temporary gap in the export-import-laws between the US and UK at that time!
This made it possible for a while to buy 'luxury cars' in the USA - and then to sell them with a huge profit in the United Kingdom. -
And of course, his mom got her desired dream of a car also.
With this starting capital, a sense of the right purpose - and equipped with endless patience and diligence, Isaac Tigrett built up a chain of 'coffee houses' of the rather special kind, together with a partner.

They became the famous *'Hard Rock Cafes'®*, which eventually turned out to be international customer magnets.

How did he create that success-story?

Mainly with one single motto, which was hung everywhere in his cafes. It read:

Love all, serve all!

And it obviously was put into practice so well that both the atmosphere and the turnover in his cafes were constantly improving.

In parallel to his business life *Isaac Tigrett* was a faithful devotee* of Sathya Sai Baba.
*Someone who gave herself or himself completely to a person or a cause, in the sense of full devotion.
But only once in many years he had a short talk with Swami, within the temple precincts in *Brindavan*, Sai Baba's second Ashram near *Bengaluru*.

Sai, cryptic as he sometimes used to be, had spontaneously approached Tigrett and then said something to him as follows:

'How good you finally arrived here!
I have been waiting for you for such a long time!'

And with these few words, quoted from memory, any personal contact between the two men was over again for many years.
But inwardly Isaac Tigrett remained with Sai Baba.
Then, one day maybe in the 1970s or 80s, the 'Hard Rock Cafe'® owner was driving his fast Porsche and was also going to parties a lot.

Unfortunately, alcohol, parties and Porsche are not such a good combination . . . Rather, one should deposit the car keys with friends before the party begins.

Isaac Tigrett, however, had kept his keys - and he drove in an inebriated state.
But when the car suddenly gave a loud crash, while it cut through the guarding rail, Isaac was all sober again!
So he and his car fell deep into a chasm of about fifty to one hundred meters to the ground.

Then, as if in slow motion Sai Baba personally 'appeared' in the co-driver's seat - and he embraced Tigrett tightly with his arms.

Next, the car hit the ground.
Like the shattering fist of a giant. It was a total wreck.
And Sai was gone.

Tigrett, however, climbed out of the mangled car almost without a scratch - which was 'not possible' for anybody, considering the height of the fall . . .

Impossible, as so many things around Sai Baba.

The Temple of Healing

Understandably, Isaac Tigrett was very grateful for this life-saving lesson and personal help, as he was for everything else that Sai Baba allowed him to do - becoming a new and responsible human being, for instance.

When Tigrett was in *Prashanti Nilayam* later on, he even received an interview at long last. At some point, Sai Baba asked members of the group present in the room:

'What is the path to God?'

Some of them tried to answer the question, but not Isaac, because - at least so he thought - he had no hunch whatsoever.
Then Swami said, smiling at Tigrett in his inimitable way:

'Love all, serve all!'

And Isaac Tigrett had his very own form of enlightenment in that moment!

Sai Baba integrated this motto into his projects, until he coined this sentence to function as the key affirmation for his entire work as well.
Tigrett, on the other hand, continued to enjoy great further success with his remarkable 'Coffee plus Food' chain of 'Hard-Rock-Cafes'. -
But at some point he had enough of it all.

Then he sold his business for estimated two hundred million Dollars - and moved on other enterprises.
Anyway, Tigrett now had this heap of money and so he journeyed - once again - to India, Puttaparthi, *Prashanti Nilayam,* the Abode of Highest Peace.
And Swami invited him for a conversation.
During this interview, he asked Sai Baba, whether he could donate part of that money to him?
And this was no rhetorical question, since Sai at times had also refused certain donations - even large ones - when the origins of those assets were improper - which Swami always was informed about.

But in Isaac Tigrett's case, Sai Baba replied:
'Let's build a hospital!'
And so it happened, that about 50-100 Million Dollars from the sale of the 'Hard-Rock-Cafes' flowed to the trusts that had been established by Sathya Sai Baba, which passed it on to the 'Larsen and Tubro' company, which had built several other major projects for Sai Baba already.
Eventually, they built the most beautiful and efficient top technology clinic of the world - according to the plans of a special British architect *Mr. Keith Critchlow,* whose professional field of interest were major spiritual and religious buildings around the globe. -
This huge temple of healing, with about three hundred beds is one of the heart pieces of Sai Baba's legacy - and it is still running and operating free of charge - a real model project for humanity!

Do we follow Sai Baba's example - or do we rather prefer to continue with cannibalism à là Cain and Abel?!
Swami is 'changing garments' right now - so it is up to us to choose which way to go! Om Sai Ram!

The amazing project of building the described Poly Clinic of the highest international care-giving level was on top of that completed within the record time of exactly one year - according to Sai Baba's announcement on the occasion of his 65th birthday on November 23rd, 1990.

The clinic, which then was opened on November 22nd in 1991, by performing four successful open-heart bypass operations, mainly treats people who, as a mother or father, have a family to support, and who could never afford an operation or expensive medical products.
For instance, heart catheter operations with 'Balloon' or 'Stent', Bypass surgery, closing heart wall defects - as in paediatrics - and meanwhile even eye and kidney surgery plus dialysis station according to the needs of the patient.

All operations and medicines, even room and boarding - plus room and boarding for the accompanying family members - are just as free as are all the treatments by the many nurses and doctors.
And they have by now - 2022 - performed thousands and tens of thousands of life-saving operations and treatments for thirty years entirely free of charge!
For exact statistics, see: www.sathyasai.org.

In addition, this clinic, which from a distance looks like a huge oriental sacral building, is constantly visited by doctors from all over the world, often even by entire operation teams, who want to learn by working in this model project.
Paused during COVID, these activities will hopefully resume soon.
If you are interested further, see for example,
Voleti, Choudary, MD - a US heart surgeon:
'Avatar Sri Sathya Sai Baba', a book where he shares his path to and with Sai Baba - and his working experiences in the new heart clinic. Reference for this book via the Sathya Sai Media Centers and at *Amazon.*
In addition to the various social model projects that we mentioned at the beginning, with schools, hospitals, water projects, *Seva* aid programs and the Sathya Sai Colleges and University - to name but a few - Sai Baba has also built two large, park-like *Ashrams*, where his visitors or devotees are housed in simple but clean and beautiful buildings and halls.
Women and men are accommodated separately in the halls, except for married couples and families, who are given a room together.

The following chapter will now cover a new theme.
It focusses on Sai Baba's attitude towards *PAS* or *Psycho-Active Substances,* which are currently in the process of a *Renaissance* in Medicine and Psychotherapy.

Sai Baba and Psycho-Active Substances or PAS

In the Ashram, any 'inebriating substances', especially alcohol and tobacco, were not allowed.
And Sai Baba was generally advising against any form of waste or abuse. -
Still, he himself chewed mildly stimulating *'Pan'* until his 60th birthday - which is a Betel nut bite that is chewed together with other psycho-active plant parts.
For his 60th birthday, however, which was celebrated by at least half a million devotees from India and all over the world - lasting with pre- and post-events for about one week - Sai Baba had given the motto:

'Ceiling on desires!'

for all speeches and events on this occasion.
In other words: 'Limitation of wishes'. - And from this point onwards he did not use 'Pan' - the Betel bite, any more - which is rather popular in India - maybe also to be a good example according to the chosen motto.

On the other hand, there are some reports that Baba once materialized a small piece of *Hashish* for a stressed manager - which never was used, of course, but kept in a shrine of worship in the family's altar room.
Furthermore, Sai, who often was teaching by way of 'little stories', named *Chinna Katha,* sometimes might indirectly have expressed an opinion on the subject of *Psycho-Active Substances* or *PAS* for short.

Changing Colours

For example with the story ***'The Glasses'***, in which a very nervous and restless man goes to a wise Saint to find some help in this.
When the Saint had heard the complaints of the man, he advised his visitor:

'Surround yourself with Green!'

Otherwise, he didn't say much any more.
The restless man then went home again, despite feeling somewhat confused.
Once he had returned, however, he immediately implemented the holy man's advice to the word.

Because now he instructed painters and gardeners to paint his house all green - and to plant greenery within it and around it on top of that.

But his nervosity and his unrest did not improve.
When he finally went again and told the Saint about his mishap, the Saint had a good laugh at first - and then said to him:

'My Dear, I was talking of green tinged glasses - and that they might do you good!' -

And with that, this *'Chinna Katha'*, this little story from Sai Baba ended already.

But what exactly was indicated by those green glasses - that could improve and heal not only restlessness and fear, yet also depression and aggression? -

That remained an open question - as well as the one, if certain 'green plants' had anything to do with it?

However, if we remember Sai Baba's previous incarnation as *Sai Baba of Shirdi*, who lived from about 1835 to 1918, we will also find that *Sathya Sai Baba* himself has announced that the circle of followers around Shirdi Sai always used to start the later evening - before they retired - sitting and chatting together.

And besides, they shared - yes, what?

Well, they smoked a *Chillum,* an Indian pipe made of clay, which contained herbs - tobacco and cannabis - and on top of the herbs, there was a small piece of opium, which was smoked also!

For more details, see *'Good Chances'* by *Howard Levin*.

Which clarifies that Shirdi Sai Baba was quite familiar with *PAS or Psycho-Active Substances!*

And one last quote from Sathya Sai Baba himself on the subject of *PAS*, to be found in:

'Bhagavan Sri Sathya Sai Baba - The Man and the Avatar' by *Prof. V. K. Gokak*, p. 221:

> I am the the pharmaceutist chemist
> Manufacturing new drugs
> For this disease called worldly life.
> You still cling
> To medicines I produced long ago.
> Come nearer!
> Let each one do his work
> With greater dedication.

Hanuman and the *Sanjeevani* Mountain at *Hill View Stadium.*

The Statue of Hanuman with the Sanjeevani Mountain

The history of this statue might provide some additional symbolic perspectives on Sai Baba's position, as far as *Psycho-Active Substances or PAS* are concerned - if we are willing to understand them that way.

It is the statue of the Indian monkey god *Hanuman*, who fights valiantly at the side of prince *Rama* and his brother, *Lakshmana* against the demons under their sinister chieftain *Ravana,* who first had abducted Rama's wife *Sita*.
As it is described in the *Ramayana* - the ancient report of the deeds of the famous Avatar and protector of the downtrodden, *Rama*.
In one of these battles - mostly against the mighty and high-standing demon Lord Ravana, who is as egotistic as he is brutal - Lakshmana, Rama's younger brother, was hit by a poisoned and lethally enchanted projectile of the demons.
No physician was able to awaken Lakshmana - who had always been inseparable from Rama - from his deep and death-like coma.
The 'Royal Physician' recommended, however, to apply special healing herbs or healing plants that were named *Sanjeevani* plants.
But the doctor added that these herbs would only restore Lakshmana's health if he could get them before the next sunrise.

Since the mountain with the Sanjeevani plants, also called *'Sanjeevani Mountain'*, was far away, Hanuman offered to fly there - and to bring back the sacred Sanjeevani herbs in time!
This he was able to do because he was the son of the 'God of the Air and Wind' *Vayu*.
But when Hanuman arrived at that mountain-range after an 'uneventful flight', he soon had found the indicated mountain - but then he was not sure which plants were the right ones.
So he decided - to simply transform into the giant aspect of Hanuman, in order to remove and take the whole *'Sanjeevani-Mountain'* and bring it back to Lakshmana.

And this feat was successful. When Rama's brother had received a preparation of the proper plants, his death-like cold and stiffness soon left him - and after a little while, Lakshmana was whole and healthy again!

So much of this fascinating myth for your background information regarding the following episode.
What did Sai Baba intend, when he gave the order in January 1990 to erect a statue of *Hanuman* carrying the *Sanjeevani-mountain?* And where?!
Above the huge *'Hill View Stadium'*, which is designed to accommodate hundreds of thousands of people at big festivals like Sai Baba's birthday.
And the statue is 65 English feet high - about 20 meters - so that this sculpture is clearly visible from all places of the stadium, as well as from far away!

Told all in all, a rather enormous effort - especially in India! But for what purpose?!
Because Sai Baba never wasted any resources.

Maybe, this statue, which shows *Hanuman* while he is flying with the *Sanjeevani Mountain*, is meant to remind us of something - but of what?
Of Hanuman's great loyalty and bravery?
Maybe also - but there are many other places in the *Ramayana* where Hanuman's brave and courageous actions are even more evident.

Therefore, as it seems, it might be more about the meaning of the 'Sanjeevani-Mountain', and with this, about *the healing plants and herbs*.

In the Rig-Veda, we find several places where healing, inner visions and God-awareness are described - when 'holy plants', such as the mysterious 'soma' were applied.
Soma may have been a mixture of cannabis, opium and psycho-active fungi.

Therefore it could be that the very Sanjeevani, which Hanuman brings back timely and in swift flight - how else? - are also containing *Psycho-Active Substances or PAS,* which are indeed often able to improve or even heal many inner injuries and other psychological 'scar formations' - which the collective, self-centered ego-ghost has left in almost all of us.

And *perhaps* this statue of Hanuman with the Sanjeevani mountain is intended to point towards the integrative and healing power inherent in certain plants and herbs, which can reverse the collective prohibition of love - with all its lethal 'collateral damages'!?

But where else is supposed to point?

Maybe. Possibly . . .

At any rate, this amazing statue was so important to Sai Baba that he himself came to the rescue, when the commissioned company had some problems with the difficult calculations of the weight distribution within this sculpture.

At that impasse, Swami simply 'materialized' a miniature replica of the statue to be erected - for the engineers who planned this challenging work of art. -

It measured about 3.5 inches, 'out of thin air', as he did so often.

This template elegantly solved the difficult problems of the engineers - for instance by showing them that the sculpture needed a pedestal to stand on - so that we later visitors can see this reminder of *Hanuman* and the *Sanjeevani* every time we go to Prashanti Nilayam now.

Om Sai Ram.

But even if we are allowed to interpret some of Shirdi and Sathya Sai Baba's actions and messages as a positive perspective on controlled and healing medical use of *Psycho-Active Substances* in psychotherapy and psycho-somatic medicine, then it still holds true that any kind of abuse and waste was a sign of ignorance and weakness of character for Sai Baba, which he advised to change.

But as far as *PAS* in the psychotherapeutic and medical sense were concerned, public discourse was still very one-sided during his lifetime - partly also in India - when UNO and WHO threw all substances, as different as they were, into 'one box' which was and still is 'criminalized' in total - which is a shame as well as a challenge for the medical profession!
In view of this erroneous legal situation, even Sai Baba may not have wanted to discuss *PAS* or *Psycho-Active Substances* more objectively and scientifically - at least not in public.
In parallel, however, we should remember Shirdi and Sathya Sai's indirect messages about PAS, as we've found above.
Now it remains to be seen, how his self-announced third incarnation *Prema Sai Baba* will take up the meanwhile changed Zeitgeist regarding useful and healing PAS.

Sathya Sai Baba, in any case, specifically had a dislike for tobacco, nicotine and alcohol. And he paid close attention to this in his university students.

Hidden Smoke

But once there was a student, who tried to smoke secretly. Sai Baba confronted him directly - but the student lied to him! What a nerve.

Next time, he smoked a cigarette behind a bush before he went into the temple to sing.

At this, Sai Baba called him to his room and confronted him again.

And when the student repeated his false claims, Sai Baba just circled his magic hand - and presto! he had materialized a photo that showed the smoking student behind the bush.

Even if self-declared Western experts know 'for sure' that such things are 'impossible' - as miracles don't fit so well with their often pre-judgemental constructivism.

Very similar as with all *PAS* or *Psycho-Active Substances* that have been used in medicine for improvement and healing for thousands of years!

But in all of those cases, the real scientist will only be convinced by the real experiment - and not by the 'blinders-mentality' of those, who decide from far away, what is - allegedly! - possible according to physics - and what is not.

Almost like with *Galileo, Copernicus* and *Kepler* - or with *Darwin, Freud, Einstein* or *Higgs*.
First, all the 'experts' were against the new paradigms.
'That can by no means be true!?' they proclaimed.
At first. And by now?
Now all these people are considered to be important scientists because of their insights!

And regarding Sai Baba, millions can confirm his amazing para-normal phenomena - not only in his personal Ashram environment, but also worldwide and in many countries.

From Sai's hands emerged watches, rings, necklaces, bracelets, photographs, documents, air-plane tickets, currency notes and fruit - including fruit that wasn't growing anywhere in India at that time - to mention but a few examples.
Sometimes, these many presents were genuine and very valuable, such as gold watches or a diamond ring, which later was estimated at about 100,000 US $ at Tiffany's in New York.

Sometimes, however, there also were cheap imitation watches, which soon quit working; or simple costume jewellery. The respective quality may at times have been a message for the people who received them.

But now something to really puzzle our positivistic and rational mind.

Because Sai frequently used to materialize - amongst the above things - even train or plane tickets!

And these tickets always were 'paid and confirmed' in the computer systems of the airlines! -
Now how to 'explain' any of these phenomena?!
On one hand 'impossible', because the airplane ticket was 'taken from thin air' by Sai Baba with a circulation of his hand - and in front of witnesses.
But on the other hand - confirmed correctly in the airline computer . . .

Do you notice, how your 'that's not possible, that must be wrong!!' sub-routines in the prejudice generators around the limbic system and in the cortex are starting up now?
Which is happening only, because you've never seen such a feat in person so far. This, however, was and is true for many new insights and inventions - see above - and should be proved or disproved in all cases by the experiment only. -

Sai Baba has manifested dozens of these experiments, each day of his life. -
But if people don't want to travel to see for themselves, then ignorance and prejudice may remain . . .
And those prejudices within the patriarchal system have lots of difficulties with the divine love, healing and empathy that could be found near Sai Baba at any given time.

Why so?

Because this radiant divine love was questioning the old paradigm of fear, hate and violence.

But in spite of this blindness in many 'rational people', who at first questioned his work, Sathya Sai Baba was a spiritual and religious example for many, many millions - perhaps billions of people - not only from India, but also for women and men from many countries of the world - and across all layers of society.

Baba's huge social works and his own tireless and diligent engagement to improve the lives of his devotees, as well as the fate of the whole of humanity, are described in detail in the thorough biographies on Sathya Sai Baba.
For instance, by *Mrs. 'Peddabottu', Mrs. Krystal and by Mrs. Baskin, Prof. Kasturi, Mr. Murthy* and *Mr. Ganapati.*

Therefore we only add a last report about one of Sai's 'miracles' here.

Strictly speaking, there even were several of them in this special case.

Metaphysics for the nuclear Physicist

One Indian person, who cautiously approached Sai Baba early in the 1970s and 1980s, was *Prof. Bhagavantam*, physicist by profession and father of the Indian atomic fission bomb. In other words, a man of pure science.

Although Sai Baba had materialized some objects in front of Prof. Bhagavantam already, the latter continued to doubt Swami's abilities.

A while later, during a car trip, the two of them were sitting on the sandy bank of a river, where they had paused.

Now Sai had asked Prof. Bhagavantam, if he would read the *Bhagavad-Gita*, a central holy scripture of the Hindus, if he would give it to him?

And when Prof. Bhagavantam agreed to this, Sai Baba took a little of the sand the river had left - and then playfully let it trickle through his empty hands.
Then he took some more sand - while he also was asking Prof. Bhagavantam to hold out his hands.

And when Baba poured the sand from his hands into Prof. Bhagavantam's hands, suddenly there also was a miniature edition of the *Bhagavad-Gita* - without any imprint of publisher or printer - and in the middle of the river sand!

Prof. Bhagavantam thanked Swami and was as moved as he was impressed - but he still had some deep lingering doubts, whether these manifestations were genuine.

Some time later, however, there was a contact between Swami and Prof. Bhagavantam, when Sai Baba once visited the professor in his office.
On his desk, he had a sheet of fresh stamps.

Then Sai Baba slowly moved his hand above the sheet of stamps - and at the same moment . . .
Prof. Bhagavantam had to look twice, before he recognized that the sheet was now entirely printed with stamps, which all had Sai Baba's picture on them!

The experience of this divine experiment removed the doubts from the physicist Prof. Bhagavantam.

But in all these demonstrations, as impressing as they were and are, Sai Baba was never concerned with any form of 'collecting followers'. -
Quite the contrary - he advised against 'advertising' for him or his mission - and lived, in obvious contrast to some other 'Gurus', a very modest life for a superhuman being that could easily have 'ruled the world', if he only had wanted to.

But Sai Baba was not so interested in the 'worldly life' or possessions - because he primarily cared about the heart of all the people who visited him!

And really *everything* he did - 'My Life is my Message!' - aimed at loosening up and dissolving the greedy ego so far inherent in mankind - and at anchoring an attitude of love and friendship instead, be it towards others or to ourselves.

Five Human Values

These *Human Values* have always been the main guiding principles, in which Sai Baba instructed his devotees:

Sathya, which means *Truth*
Dharma, that is *Righteousness*
Ahimsa, denoting *Non-violence*
Prema, which sings *Love* and
Shanti, that eventually brings *Peace.*

Sai Baba never got tired of recommending and repeating these fundamental *Human Values - HV* for short - as a safe and useful compass for our life.
But we often have heard very similar 'recommendations' from rather authoritarian persons - priests, teachers, politicians and so on, who are 'recommending' a lot - but way too frequently don't follow their 'own advice'!

What a different world around Sai Baba!
Because he was a walking incarnation of these virtues, which he, however, taught less by always exactly fitting recommendations, but even more by his own example of always being active for others. - Directly and 'From Heart to Heart', as he often used to say.
Sai Baba was *Love in Action* all his life - and he still is, in myriad ways, but most visibly by way of his institutional heritage, which continues to provide education and health care for thousands, while inspiring millions year for year.

Any education in Sai Baba's schooling and training institutes is always implemented as *Educare.* -
That is a caring and spiritual form of education, which, in addition to learning various contents and skills - and achieving the goals in class - always places the above mentioned *Five Human Values* right at the center of most lessons in the different subjects.

Because pupils and students without ethics and without spiritual or religious roots are later on in life often like ships without a proper anchor.
Then they are tossed around by the storms of the transient material world - and could easily be endangered to go 'shipwrecked' - without the compass and anchor of a socially and spiritually oriented life.

A bit above, we just found the 'compass' of these main *Five Human Values* that we still remember.
In addition to this basic equipment or compass, Sai Baba always advised to stay firmly rooted in one's original religious tradition. -
But at the same time, he used to welcome everybody who visited him. Accordingly he often said things like:

'Theists, atheists, atheistic theists and theistic atheists alike: I welcome them all, love them all and serve them all!
An open mind, a truthful character and a heart that is willing to learn are quite enough! -
Because it is the Heart that reaches the Goal!'

In very similar terms, Sai Baba frequently addressed people of all different 'faiths' and walks of life.
He invited them to examine him and his work closely - and then to learn and profit from all of it at one's own discretion.
Or maybe not - for instance, if the 'right time' or simply the courage to do so is missing - or has at least been missing *so far*.

At the same time, Sai makes it quite clear what the real intentions of his super-human work are:
He gives us a lot of what we hope for - such as healings, 'miracles' of all kinds, objects for a spiritual connection, progress in our family, in our education and professions, as well as prosperity and an open heart for nature. -
And he does this to awaken our inner yearning to get that from him for which he really arrived here on earth to give it to us.
And that is ultimately the most valuable present, the ground-breaking and heart-opening transformation by Sai into mutually loving and serving human beings.

An attitude he incorporated far beyond what is usual and possible in a normal human life.
And just this profound transformation - from hardened, stressed and aggressive ego-minded people into their very opposite - in which Sai Baba step by step furthers the blooming of Love in the hearts of many millions of human beings - that is the real 'miracle' of this true God in human form.

Because 'Magic people' with quite impressive paranormal abilities - including 'materializations' - do exist, here and there, throughout the ages - even now, several of them, worldwide. And they appear especially in India.

But never in this awesome fullness of divine powers.

And - most important - never connected with this kind of global and sustainable change towards love and cooperation within the heart and soul of many millions or even billions of people!

Sai Baba - as the Divine Mother and the Divine Father - is the first cosmic parent-person of humanity, who now was accessible to so many people - because of all the modern media and today's flight travel possibilities.

And he was the first *Avatar*, who has been able to guide uncounted human beings to a timely update of their personality towards a loving attitude - and this during his own lifetime already. The fruits and further consequences of Sai Baba's lifelong activities will probably be appreciated only in future years in their full impact and meaning for humanity.

And this holds true especially, since we still have to include *Prema Sai Baba* and his actions later on.

According to Sathya Sai Baba's own prediction, as we've seen before.

By the way, already Shirdi Sai Baba, who left his mortal coils in 1918, predicted some time before he died, the year and the place of his next incarnation - which was to be eight years after his own death and in Southern India.

Accordingly, *Sathya Sai Baba* was born in 1926 - and now where did this happen? Well, in Southern India, in the town *Puttaparthi*, near Bangalore, today Bengaluru.

And there is a number of devotees, who personally had known Shirdi Sai Baba and who - when they later came to Sathya Sai Baba - tried to 'test' this new and so 'completely different' Guru.

However, it was only Sathya Sai Baba, who always tested his 'old devotees'.

He did so by telling them events pertaining to memories they had, which only Shirdi Sai Baba could have known, since no one else was around when those things were happening at that time.

And so they finally realized that their former Shirdi Sai Baba had now indeed transformed for them into this smiling, young and radiant Sathya Sai Baba!

So far, we have attempted to better understand some prominent aspects of Sathya Sai Baba's personality and of his epoch-initiating works.

But now, as we are slowly getting closer to the end of this chapter, we would like to focus on a further aspect of Sai Baba's message which might well be one of the most significant - if this idea is permitted, regarding all the other superlatives in Baba's work and life.

The point we're talking about is Sai Baba's message of unity and equality between all religions.

A special Sarva Dharma Symbol*

*Of the ***Sri Sathya Sai International Organization*** until 1997.
It includes six religions; clockwise from top: Hindu, Buddhist, Zoroastric, Mosaic, Islamic and Christian faith.
The stylized Sarva Dharma Column in the middle shows the just opening Unifying Lotus of Love.

Good pictures of the original
Sarva Dharma Aikya Stupa in Prashanti Nilayam
can be found on the Internet.

The Sarva Dharma Stupa

If we look at our human religious history, which so far often employs mutual devaluation - like 'pagans' or 'disbelievers' - and wars amongst religions, this message of religious equality and cooperation by the Avatar of this age is a new invitation.
An invitation to dare a real, power blocks and continents connecting ecumenical movement of all religions. -
And probably one of the most obvious evolutionary 'quantum leaps' beyond the often incrusted positions of creed in our mostly so 'exclusive' religions!
While we are in this context on the mutual equality and basic identity of all religions - let's have a closer look at a special symbol really worth seeing in the *Ashram* of Sathya Sai Baba in Puttaparthi.
There, in *Prashanti Nilayam*, abode of Peace Supreme, it happened that Sathya Sai Baba had ordered a sculpture, a holy symbol for the unity in duality and also for eternal life, to be built in the Ashram, in 1975.
Around the base of that pillar there also were five-sided foundations with water pools, while the pentagonal and therefore also five-sided column rose from the center of those water pools.*
At the very top, the column is crowned by a just opening lotus flower. It is easy to imagine that the original water ponds with their faucets and fountains symbolized the feminine aspect - while the pillar in the middle embodies the masculine principle.

*In ancient *Sanskrit*, a sacred *Yoni Lingam Stupa* as well.

The point is now that five tables are attached at the base of the column, which are depicting and describing some of the religions of the world - one plaque on each of the five sides - so that every side of the pentagonal column always corresponds to one specific religion.

These five religions are: Hinduism, Zoroastrianism, Islam, Buddhism and Christianity.

So far, so fine, so beautiful, one may say, the helpful path towards the 'Unity of Religions' - which is a good intention! -

But those religions would first have to participate in this approach of mutual recognition!
Certainly, a very justified objection.

And if we take a closer look at the ***Sarva Dharma Stupa*** - as this pillar is fittingly named, because its meaning is: ***Universal Righteousness Column*** - such 'objections' are visible there in a symbolic form already. -

Because Sai Baba knew very well that the established religions partly had some rather immature and inflexible religious ideas of patriarchal nature, which usually were claimed to be the 'only truth'.
That could be one of the reasons, why this lotus-bud, which crowns the pillar, is only just about to open itself.
And something else almost 'hits' the eye.
This entire column is of grey colour!

Dear Readers, to understand the inner meaning of this colour, you need to have some background information, if you haven't been to *Prashanti Nilayam* before. -

Which is, that in this *Ashram* of Sathya Sai Baba virtually all the buildings - except for the Museum and Administration Buildings that are located further away from the Ashram - are painted in shining light colours!

Mainly in a gentle but radiant blue, red and yellow and mostly in pastel shades, that match very well with the greenery and blossoms of the trees, bushes and gardens that have been planted all over the Ashram.

And now this, the 'Sarva Dharma Stupa' of all places, the one column that reminds us of *Sarva Dharma*, of the importance of *'Universal Righteousness'* within the religions of the world - and now that especially is kept in grey only?!
Obviously, we can only make personal assumptions about this choice of colour by Sai Baba - but doesn't that rather intentional 'grey' of this Stupa point in-directly at the 'grey' - and often even very 'grey' misdevelopments of many overly 'monocular' and paternal religions?!

And this grey might point to the primal misdevelopment, in which almost all religions are still far too wrapped up with the original paternal religion of mankind, which is the 'religion' of all material possessions, of power and of violence up to war between religions and nations.

And it is only when enough people in those religions are ready to renounce the blood-shed and power-grabbing frenzy of this most archaic religion - that the obsolete cannibalism between men is finally going to end. -

Which will unlock a lot of power for new endeavours in society, like for the better and more equal integration of women - for a clean-up and repair of our climate and our planet - for help projects to support the self-build-up of the many developing countries - and also for the joy of a colourful life - especially in all of the main religions of our world.
And it's good to remember in this context, that this special *'Lotus Column'* in grey, which was dedicated to the *Eightfold Yogic Path* and to five of the most wide-spread religions of the world, originally was built as a symbol that unites the female and male aspect.

Later, the space around the pillar was now used for new buildings - but although the column remained, there was hardly anything left of the fountains and water pools that had been around the base, when the construction work was finished. Why so? Maybe as a mirror?
Perhaps for the more paternal religions, where symbols of the number zero and of the feminine principle have also mostly been covered by concrete?

But what did Sai Baba do later on?
Eventually, in 2001, he ordered his own new residence, *Yajur Mandir,* to be built arround that pillar!

Just like Sai, the divine mother, who gently embraces and transforms those paternally and violently 'frozen' religions with her unconditional and unlimited motherly love!

This 'grey' of the 'Lingam-column' may also depict the still frequent 'taboo' on sexuality - and homosexuality.

And it might point at the exclusion and devaluation of women that still exists in many societies and religions of this world.

Sometimes we almost felt, as if we were quietly hearing Sai Baba's voice, when we just stood there and looked at the Sarva-Dharma-Column.

'Maybe one day there will be a celebration of all forms of loving intimacy, but also of joy, family and peace - and that might be, when this Sarva-Dharma pillar is allowed to be colourful as well - at least sometimes!
Then the fountains and water pools can flow forth again also, as illuminated rainbows - similar to the spring of love in your hearts!'*

*In recent years, there have been several laser-light-shows in *Prashanti Nilayam* in beautiful colours, which included the Sarva-Dharma Stupa. That is a good omen for the future!

To be sure: This is only our intuition of what Sai Baba *could* have said by way of this Sarva Dharma Column. -

But what do we as human beings and as humanity want *for* our own religions - and what *from* our religions in the next millennium?

And what is maybe 'way too grey' or 'walled up' in our own traditions? -
And where in our religions could we possibly use some fresh colouring and renovation - plus repair of the pipes for the fountains and water-ponds?

Please notice well that this only indicates the option for a further evolutionary process in all of us - and towards a more cooperative and loving future for humanity.

But we should understand that Sai Baba's invitation to realize this option is a *New Evangelion* or *Gospel* - it is the *Good Message of Our Age*, which we should read and share together with the other *'Great Books'* from the religions of our world.

Still, Sai Baba remained quite consistent throughout his life in stating that he had not come to this earth to found any new religion.

Instead, his actions as well as his message vitalized all existing traditions of this kind in such a new way, 'that a Moslem can be a better Moslem, a Buddhist a better Buddhist and a Christ a better Christ - and so forth, for all religions - and the sooner the better!'

But when Sai Baba once was asked, whether a devotee of Sai shouldn't better pray to Sai Baba 'first' - and to Christ only in the second place . . . ?

Baba replied on the spot: 'No, no! Same, same!
This is all the same!'

And often he explained: 'You are free to call me by any name given to God - and I will hear you!'

Because only the lived equality and peace among our religions can form the solid basis for trust, love and peace in the 'worldly exchange' between the states and nations of the global community.

Meanwhile, this seems to be understood in some of the European Schools as well, where classes could be seen on TV, who were discussing the themes:
'Allah, God and the Big Bang'.

The spiritual integration work in this class of young teenagers with their engaged teacher was really impressive to behold.

The way in which the pupils were introduced to the first and last questions of our traditional religions - compared with the 'modern scientific world view' - and to see, how the disciples soon learned to behave with an increased mutual respect and appreciation - all of this was a very inspiring experience!

Perhaps with a similarly open-minded attitude towards the seemingly so 'different' or even 'impossible' feats and accomplishments of Sathya Sai Baba, we will also succeed in accepting his ancient and yet eternally new invitation:
'Love all, Serve all!'
Even if this doesn't appear to be an easy exercise for us, with our overly belligerent traditions - and plans . . . *
*Update March 2022: Russia's war against Ukraine, e.g.!

And at first sight, 'Doomsday' actually seems to be so much 'simpler' - rather than to finally learn how we can be a loving and life-oriented human family?
But what do you think about that?!

In this context we should remember that Sai Baba has constantly pointed out the importance of an internal way of practice.
In *Sanskrit*, the ancient Indian language of the *Vedas*, those methods of the inner path are often summarized as *Sadhana*.

Sadhana, the 'true way of inner transformation', implies all activities or non-activities, which guide us to our Self - to the deepest core of our soul.

And Sathya Sai Baba has even dedicated an entire book to this inner approach, using *Sadhana* as the title.

Sadhana

And also when we read the *'Autobiography of a Yogi'* by *Paramhamsa Yogananda*, we find a lot of information about this path - in a specific way, the *Kria Yoga*.

Still, all the *Great Orienters* and holy empathic souls, like Sai, Yogananda, Mohammed, Moses or Christ, to name but a few of those parents of humanity - have pointed out that the loving and serving attitude and behaviour is our first and foremost duty.

Before any Sadhana or path inside. - Only when we have done that, we can find time for Yoga, Tai-Chi or the Five Tibetans and - prepared accordingly, for concentration, contemplation, prayer and heartfelt prayer - as well as for forms of meditation and deeper awareness.

Which basically is an old wisdom that we could learn from many Christian nuns or monastery brothers as well. Such as *David Steindl-Rast* for instance, who wrote the beautiful book: *'A listening Heart'.*

Sai Baba sometimes said things like:
'If you meditate and your neighbour has a misfortune or gets sick and calls out for help - then it is your 'foremost meditation' to go there and to help as well as you can!'
'Seva first, Sadhana next!' meaning:
'Service to your neighbour first -
only then your way of spiritual exercise'!

If some of what we are saying here sounds a bit odd to you - we certainly do understand that.
Because, who really needs *Seva* and *Sadhana* in our *Meta-Morphing®* 'modern world'?
And isn't our current motto:
'Catch as catch can?!' - Or is it really??

Yes, in this case we would rather say: 'Maybe not?!'
Because the issue here it is not only the current motto, but even more the 'current currency'!

How that? Well, as already considered before:
All material 'currencies' including platinum and gold, but also diamonds - or shares and notes in all currencies of the world - be it on Cayman Islands, in Switzerland or in 'nuke-safe'? bunkers - anything material - even land, power, position and wealthy family - is what?

Most likely, we will receive - from a total amount of one thousand people, about 999 times:
'Grooovyyy - I want that also!!' as an answer. -
And is that so surprising now? -
One would perhaps sing along?!
But no, this is no surprise at all! Because most of us have been materially indoctrinated or brain-washed like that.
But one person - probably a child - might say:
'Yes, well - but all of this is going to end!
Nothing remains of it! This is what my angel explained to me - in the evening, while praying.

And she said that it is much more important to love and to care for one another. -
Rather than to 'make' too much money, only to go on to quarrel and kill each other because of 'the money', 'the land' and 'the power'.

And she - my angel - has said that all religions, which need to devalue other people and their religions - or even call for war against each other - are in truth only playing material 'catch as catch can!' also. -
Which means: 'Take as much as you can get!'
And in the end she still added that all these many overly militant 'religions' should now finally be renovated in the spirit and by the soul of love!

But the 999 others in the group of a thousand - presumably 'grown-ups' - would explain to the 'child' that there are no angels, really.
And that 'everyone must fend for themselves'. . . and after a while - kindergarten, school system and job - the child will believe that also.

Sathya Sai Baba, however, makes it very clear to us, that any form of superfluous possessions - especially, if they have been 'acquired' in a questionable way that is damaging to others - can only pull us down.
'Properties are no proper ties!' he often used to say.
In other words:

'It is not good to be too attached to ownership!'

By the way, even the old and meanwhile quite legendary *John D. Rockefeller,* who had become a multi-billionaire with his Standard Oil and 'other things', had the opportunity to experience this truth.

During all his endless 'success' while 'catching of money', he had become ever weaker and sicker - and no doctor could help him!

Only when a rather courageous doctor eventually dared to explain to Rockefeller that he had to share his wealth, in order to get healthier, he finally reacted.

Now he created a whole series of social foundations and non-profit trusts - and while his many uncounted assets became a little less, Rockefeller's personality ripened - a whole lot!

And when most doctors had already given up on him - he now was getting healthier and stronger, because of his new social, friendly and loving initiatives!

Even the judicial dismantling of his oil monopoly - yes, there were things like that back then - was meanwhile taken with humour by 'Rocky', the 'ultra rich'. -
Something that would have made him sit brooding for weeks in his office - in the times before his inner change.

But what had really happened?

Rockefeller senior had - at least in part - accomplished the huge quantum leap from a pure egomaniac capitalist to a - yes! - helpful *Stakeholder of Humanity* - and it is a development of this kind, which truly counts and lasts in our life. -
Which often makes people contented or even happy.

Because this is Sathya Sai Baba's main lesson to us:
The only currency, that is going to last - even eternally - is love alone!
And when we leave our body, we might not be asked for our account and titles - but simply:
'Where and how have we been able to love - and where and how did we miss out on that?'

For it is only along this axis that our deepest personality or soul is maturing - during and beyond the beautiful dance of our re-incarnations - if 'such a thing' were possible at all?

Eventually, this whole book about Sai Baba is none other than an invitation to these three endeavours:
Seva, Sadhana and *Tantra* - meaning a loving flow at work, in the inner and outer relation to God and in erotic intimacy - all of which radiate positively into the family and into the surrounding society as well!

And Sai Baba often called this loving flow - which just might be what life is all about - by a specific acronym, which spells:

CIA* and is short for *Constant Integrated Awareness.

It hinted at an ongoing presence even during our worldly performance - and that we can achieve it in our lives.

But if we want this constant connection to the source of love in our soul and our middle, then we are also well advised to develop according to the afore mentioned *Five Human Values* - by including them into our own lived and self-experienced reality.

And you can even check that for yourself, if you'd like.
Try it out:
For instance, with the following 'mental exercise'.

Just imagine . . .

CAUTION! CAVE!
The first part of his exercise is not intended for seriously depressive or otherwise psychologically challenged or handicapped people!
If you are not sure about that, you better go straight to the second part of the exercise.

Now here is the - difficult - first part.
For one week you do 'business as usual' - with the inner attitude: 'Life is dangerous and full of enemies, whom you must either escape or defeat!
Work is always maximum hard and totally exhausting - and accordingly, loving closeness and intimacy are almost impossible to find. -
It is only a question of power and money in this life - and besides, as you can see on TV every day - we soon seem to be headed for terminus anyway . . . so why should we exert ourselves any more?

This life here is all coincidence anyhow - and in the end, we can change nothing at all . . .'

Now use these 'inner beliefs' for one week -
If you absolutely want to do this for so long! -
A week at work, with family and friends - and also with yourself, always accompanied by the mentioned 'beliefs' or, in this case, rather prejudices, which can also be summarized under: 'Life is hard and vicious!' -

And we must also be like that to fight our way through - each against the other - and evolution against all!'

And then observe during this week how your mind and your mood are doing.

But someone might wonder: 'Observe my mood'?
Aren't you moody?! Mostly I think and know, you know.
And every now and then - just recently! -
I think I've got 'a feeling' - but then my wife says to me:
'No, no - you've only thought it all up!
And I still should check on my mood and mind?'

Sure. All thoughts, feelings, pictures, ideas - that appear in the mirror of your inner mind - simply observe them, while you are percolating the attitude:
'Life is hard, but at least unjust, too!'

And when you're done with this strange first part of the exercise, here is part two.

'The same thing the other way round'.
Meaning:
One week with the faith that we are all part of families small and large - and that the Family of Humankind is a concern essential enough for the ancient beings that are the 'Parents of Humanity', so they constantly incarnate as those *Parentars,* in order to loosen up and finally dissolve the rampant blindness and ignorance of the greedy and violent ego in us. -

If we care for this to happen.

Because it is the basic loving character of these *Great Ammas* and *Avatars*, which teaches us an attitude that makes even the most difficult work or task a bit easier to accomplish. -

With that, help and support are often appearing 'as if by themselves' in our life, when we ourselves start giving whatever our talents make possible to share.

Back to the set of beliefs for the second part
- and week - of the exercise.

'The people in my life are important to me - therefore I prefer to consider everybody, as far as possible, as co-players, with whom I can share validation, respect and equality. -
This goes for the profession, for the outer family and for my inner family.

Closeness, intimacy and love are possible - everywhere in life and 'even' in the partnership or marriage!

And finally, we all are incarnations and investigations of love - just like this whole amazing creation - and we are allowed to be a tiny yet important part of this infinite and autopoetic evolution.
What a cosmic present by this Divine Love!'

And then, as explained, you go for one week - or as long as you want - with an inner posture according to the live-shaping beliefs that are based on love, communion and communication.

And it might also be good to take a few short notes in the evening during each of those exercises - both in the 'negative' and the 'positive' phase.

This can help you to find out, why Sathya Sai Baba's main messages were centered on *Seva*, selfless service - *Sadhana*, the spiritual path to the inner self - and *Tantra*, which is loving intimacy - to such a degree.

But for Sai Baba this was always synonymous for:
'Engage yourselves!' - that is:

'Get involved - in your society, at work, in your families!
Only like this will your love fully blossom.'

Dear Readers, please remember in this context:

beautiful
Many roads lead to Rome -
but elsewhere, it is also

Find your own way - and if you want, ask yourself from time to time:

'And how about Love?'

As we have hinted at in the beginning already, this book about Sathya Sai Baba is of course at best a first and very tentative approach to this trans-millennia phenomenon.

But he is showing humankind the way of cooperation and love in the most difficult moment - just when our blind and egomaniac self-destruction seems imminent.

'Love all, serve all!'
is his clarion call, which probably is the only viable way out of this repetitive compulsion of violence and war.

And if there is any hope for a cooperative, united and Loving Humanity in our common future, then we should recognize that we owe this, prior to anybody else, to one person only.

And that is *Sri Sathya Sai Baba*. And beyond, also to the Trinity of Shirdi, Sathya and Prema Sai Baba!

Therefore we feel that this book certainly is the most meaningful of our writings, because here, beyond all limited human possibilities, it becomes very clear that the absolute Principle of Love in the form of 'Godhuman Parents' is not leaving us alone - but they personally appear and share our life! -

While reminding us of our very first birthright, of our right to love - others and ourselves.

Therefore we are cherishing Sai Baba's eternal work and remain in deep gratitude for his divine song:

'Ceiling on desires!'

'Help ever, hurt never!'

'Love all, serve all!'

Middle: **Shirdi Sai Baba**
Left: **Sathya Sai Baba** Right: **Prema Sai Baba**

The inspiring Interview

And now, at long last, back to that rather grey and fresh October morning in the year 2000.
Musing inwardly, how likely any 'good luck' might be on such a chilly morning, the author of these lines, Anselm, pulled his garments closer, while wandering towards the temple-compound in the half darkness of the very early morning.
The evening before had surprised us with some new and interesting developments. Meaning that several people from Germany, who had been to the *Ashram* for a while, were leaving - and had offered to pass on their scarves with German colours, so that future visitors from there, who didn't have any, could use them.
They had given us the number of their apartment, so the scarves could be picked up at their place that evening.

On the other hand, fate would have it that Gabriele had met with two newly arrived women from Germany during afternoon *Darshan* that day. And they were quite interested in forming a small German group with us - but didn't have any scarves with German colours.
When we had considered these synchronous events in our apartment for a moment, Gabriele went to collect the 'German scarves' from the devotees that were about to leave the next day.
And she had those scarves with her, when she set out for *Darshan* in the half-dark of that unusually cold and rainy Indian morning in October.

Then Anselm was sitting in meditation on the men's side, waiting for Swami to appear and walk by.
As he was placed in one of the further away lines, he now kept all his attention on Sai, who had meanwhile begun giving *Darshan* on the women's side.

At this point, Anselm was thinking: 'If we could only bring an organized German group together, one of these days - dreaming is always allowed, isn't it?!'

But while he was pondering this, his glance briefly went from the sweet form of the approaching 'Love in Action' over to the colourful temple with its wide veranda of white marble, in front of which the many white-clad students of Swami's University were forming their lines.

Then he looks back at Baba again, who is slowly getting ever closer now. -
But hadn't somebody been up there, on top of that veranda - perhaps waving to a person in the crowd?

Until he realizes that it is Gabriele, his wife, who is standing there - waving to himself, so he can join that German group, which just has been called for an interview by Sai Baba!

'Which group is that supposed to be?' Anselm thought - but at Gabriele's persistent waving on the temple-veranda, he slowly got up and began walking towards her, safely guided by some supportive guards.

What had happened before on the women's side, was the timely transfer of the German group scarves from Gabriele to the newly arrived visitors. -

And those were fortunate enough not only to sit in the very 'first line' that fresh October morning in South India - but they even were blessed by Swami's: 'Go!'
for an interview that also included our whole, instantly formed group of four Germans.
If our memory is correct on that number.

Then, all of us were waiting there, on the veranda of the temple; women and men were separate as usual, and we sat there together with several Indians, who also had a younger couple amongst them.

The time of energized anticipation seemed to last forever, while Swami still was giving *Darshan* to the people on the men's side.

Handing over a bundle of letters, Sai Baba approached us now, while he exchanged a word here and there with the staff of the Ashram, plus of the various schools and colleges and of the university - of the Sri Sathya Sai Institute of Higher Learning and Medical Sciences.

Then the Divine Being in human form was right next to us - and with the gentlest smile he spoke to us:

'Yes, now about your group - please, come inside!'

Then he waited at the door for greetings, as a polite host will do, until everybody had slowly entered the medium-sized interview room.
Now all of us, maybe ten to fourteen people, had settled on the floor, again women and men separate.

Then Swami entered the room also, closing the door, while a helper switched on the fan, which immediately was approved by Sai Baba with a: 'Well done!' or so.

Before we could think of anything else, Baba manifested a somewhat larger amount of *Vibhuti,* of healing ash, which was distributed amongst the women right away.
Then he swiftly walked over to his chair.
Mind you, Dear Reader, that Swami had walked the earth for almost 75 years at that time, which meant day for day in constant service to humanity. -

And that, although his body had suffered a number of rather severe diseases and some accidents in the past.
Despite all this, Sai Baba seemed as agile as a youngster, as he floated to his chair.

And never have we felt more at home than in the vivid and sparkling aura of Sai, as he sat down now - to begin the exchange with our group.
While we were still digesting the amazing fact of that manifestation from 'nowhere' under our very eyes, we suddenly realized that Sai Baba next went on by asking a question that surprised both of us.

This turn of events requires some additional background information.

During the months prior to our journey to India, we had composed a collection of poems and texts that had been written by Anselm and typed by Gabriele into a first and barely presentable text, parts of which were in English.

When we had reached the *Ashram* later on, we took that text of maybe forty pages with us to each *Darshan*, with our prayers to Swami to bless it.
But it never happened - too many visitors, plus our lines weren't amongst the first ones . . .

Tough luck, we thought.
But then we realized that wishing for Sai Baba's special blessing during *Darshan* was simply one more of those attachments to let go of.

As a result, both of us had written a letter to Baba with our personal issues, which we intended to send to him by mail, together with a copy of the text that we have mentioned above.
The day before the Interview - and not knowing about it at all! - we extra had been to one of the tiny super-markets in *Puttaparthi,* to acquire a somewhat bigger manila envelope that would hold our letters and also the typed manuscript.
Also, we had gotten the necessary stamps, so everything could be sent to Swami by Indian mail service.

And that whole package was sitting in the middle of the table in our apartment, with the firm intention to mail it at the postal station after this morning *Darshan.*

Instead, we were all surprised to be gratefully enjoying Swami's interview now!
And Anselm had brought a second copy of that text with poems and essays to the *Darshan* hall, which he had taken with to the interview. When he entered the room, he had left the stapled sheaf of pages near the door, so they wouldn't be in the way, as we had planned to send the parcel later on anyhow.

But Swami had other plans.
His astonishing question to Anselm was: 'What is this?' while he was indicating towards the door.
Still, Anselm didn't get it.
Only when Swami had gone on to repeat his: 'What is this?' one more time - while Gabriele and some others visibly pointed towards the manuscript left next to the door, things finally clicked for him.

Then Anselm quickly got up, got the text and handed it to Swami. While we were watching in a state of rapt attention, how Swami was looking at our texts, Anselm eventually mustered the courage to answer Sai's initial question by saying:
'Swami, this is the beginning of a book!' which resulted in a friendly smile in the Divine face, that was surrounded by the impressive halo of black hair.

And then, Baba paged through this very early and rather incomplete manuscript so diligently that we almost held our breath - even the German parts!
Now and then he chuckled a little, or he read a certain page with special concentration.
Then, without any spoken comment, but with a smile that held the power of the sun, Sai Baba gave the bundle of pages back to Anselm.

And while we were still struggling to understand what had just happened, Sai gently went on to talk to one of the women in the group.
He asked her: 'Where is your band?!'
At this, the woman looked a bit confused, until someone whispered into her ear:
'Husband!!' Now she understood - but her answer was:
'Well, Swami, I have no husband!'
Now Sai Baba looked at her directly and proclaimed:
'Next time you'll be here with your husband!' which left half a smile and a big question mark on the face of this woman.
Then Swami got really busy working with all of us who were present in that group.
He talked at length with some Indian men, who seemed to be business leaders or doctors, but this was in Telugu or Hindi, which we didn't understand.
Then Sai Baba selected some devotees from the group to talk individually and in private in the adjacent smaller room with them, which was separated from the larger group interview room only by a curtain.

During this pause, we tried to sort out what was just happening. What did this text-episode mean?

But now Swami was back again, and next he invited the young Indian couple to the other room.
This time, the discussion next door was quite lively, and sometimes peals of laughter could be heard through the curtain between the two rooms.

Then Sai Baba emerged again, holding the curtain to the side, so the chuckling couple in his tow could join our larger circle again.

An eternal moment later, Swami pointed at the two of us, Gabriele and Anselm, to walk over to the small room!

Awestruck, we sat down on a small bench next to the wall in this modest room that was mainly furnished with Sai Baba's chair in the middle, plus some mats and pillows on the floor and a shelf or two on the side.

For a while we waited there, hearing how Sai was now speaking to the others.
Then he suddenly opened the curtain and looked at us.
First, he smiled at us with his endlessly caring eyes - but when he saw us sitting on that bench near the wall, he told us:
'Oh, no - please, sit nearer, over here!'
And with these words he went to his chair, indicating the pillows on the floor right next to him with his hands.

Right next to Him, the *Poorna-Avatar* of our age!
It seemed that our hearts and our feet were stumbling a bit, as we followed his friendly invitation, until we finally managed to sit at Swami's feet.

Directly at his feet! And with that, immediately in this loving divine Aura that ended all yearning and made the air sparkle with life - where we were allowed to bask for a long while of eternity - just Sai Baba and the two of us.

Questions and answers on spiritual as well as personal and professional issues went back and forth with ease, as we enjoyed this rejuvenating flow of Divine Love.

And for some time, Sai Baba entered into an intricate discussion with Gabriele, explaining, advising and exhorting her - always with that friendly twinkle in the eye, while all the love of the Mother-Goddess was showered on her in plenty.
At some point, while indicating Anselm, Gabriele said to Swami: 'This is my husband!'

And Sai responded: 'Yes! I know him!'

What blessing! Both of us felt completely at home and on Cloud Nine . . .

Maybe to ground us a bit after this 'stint in heaven', Swami got more serious towards the end - and then admonished us in no uncertain terms: 'Do your duty!'

But when we felt humbled by the suddenly flaming gaze of the Avatar, he quickly brought out his hospitable and jovial smile again, while he was guiding our way back to the other room now, where the group was waiting.

Making some remarks here and there, Swami suddenly went over to a desk in a corner.

Then we saw, how the slender person clad in orange gently selected a letter from one of the stacks there.

A Letter and a Song

While was Swami returning to us, he briefly scanned it - and then looked at us with his beautiful impish smile.
'See who wrote to the Ashram!'
His beaming face seemed to indicate.
And then, all of us there in the circle were completely stunned to realize that we were looking at the stationary, seal and signature of one of the most elevated offices in east and west on this planet!
Only the short text of the letter remained all covered by Sai Baba's hand.
What a friendly and far-reaching revelation. -
Sai's followers can be found on any level, everywhere.

Although this unusual sign of Swami's grace indicated that the interview might soon be ending, which caused a small stirring in the group, Sai Baba still had some other plans for us.
Again, he sat down on his chair in the larger interview room.
Then he looked at us, always one person after the other and directly in the eye.
Finally, he asked with a questioning smile:
'Love is my Form?'
It only took us some moments - then we understood.
Sai wanted to sing with us!
After this longer exchange with each one of us and at his advanced age - but he still wanted to do that!
And so did all of us - first shyly, then with gusto.

Here are the lines of this song:
Love is my Form
Swami = S *Circle = C*
S: Love is my form, truth is my breath, bliss is my food.
C: Love is my form, truth is my breath, bliss is my food.

S: My life is my message, expansion is my life.
C: My life is my message, expansion is my life.

S: No season for love, no reason for love,
No birth no death.
C: No season for love, no reason for love,
No birth no death.

S: Prema Sathya Ananda, Dharma Shanti Ananda.
C: Prema Sathya Ananda, Dharma Shanti Ananda.

S: Shirdi Sai Sathya Sai Prema Sai Jai Jai,
Shirdi Baba Sathya Baba Prema Baba Jai Jai,
Love is my form, truth is my breath, bliss is my food.
C: Shirdi Sai Sathya Sai Prema Sai Jai Jai,
Shirdi Baba Sathya Baba Prema Baba Jai Jai,
Love is my form, truth is my breath, bliss is my food.

Om Shanti, Shanti, Shanti.

By the time the last notes of this heart-warming song had faded away, all in this group felt transported to a supreme plane of existence, protected by the blanket of Swami's infinite love.

A quiet moment followed.
But then, Sai Baba was already addressing us again:
'Be happy!' he told us with a big smile.
At this, we - Gabriele and Anselm - briefly looked at each other. Evidently a sentence to remember, as we had heard this invitation to happiness from Sai Baba in the other room also, when just the two of us were with him.

For a moment, we pause the report of our interview with Swami here, to mention an incident that once had happened in another interview and was published later.

Inside your Mind
In that group, there was a woman, who was afflicted by those 'Sai Baba is only for the rich' ideas - and therefore she was nourishing some doubts.
And these doubts of hers seemed only to be confirmed, when Swami turned to a business magnate as the very next thing in that interview.

And this woman thought: 'Didn't I know it!
There he goes again - he is only for the rich!'

But she had hardly finished that thought, when Sai Baba cut his last sentence to the business leader short, turned around to her and explained in similar terms:

'Well, you see, Dear One - if Sai can change the attitude in someone at the helm, then this means improvements for many families who are working for that person.

And that is one of the main reasons, why Swami is taking good care of the rich, also.
Also - but not only, if you perceive Sai's ongoing efforts for the poor and downtrodden!'

An event that illustrates Sai Baba's all-knowing aspect, while helping us to understand his ways of working at the same time.

Now we go back to our personal, slowly ending interview with Sai Baba in October 2000.
After some further clarifying remarks for several persons in the group, Swami suddenly and nimbly got up from his chair and walked in the middle of our circle.

Standing there, with his palm downwards, he now began a spiralling movement of his right hand, while all of us held our breath.

Now a round and golden shining object appeared under his hand, which immediately was caught by Sai Baba in mid-air.
He showed the freshly manifested ring to all of us and then gave it to a devotee in the group.

And when this had just been accomplished - Swami did it again!
And a different, beautiful ring appeared from nowhere, while all of us were filled with gratefulness that we were allowed to witness these 'impossible feats'.

In addition to all those wonders, Sai Baba now went next to the two of us - and found very friendly words and gestures to bless our marriage, which caused our hearts and eyes to flow over with love . . .

Finally, Swami began to say good-bye to every person in the group. This was done in two steps, once inside the room, with a word or smile - plus second outside, on the veranda of the temple.

And in full view of those thousands of devotees, who were all sitting in front of the temple - ladies left, gents right - in silent meditation.

During the brief farewell words inside, Gabriele still was fortunate enough to receive one last and very personal: 'Be happy!' by the gentle voice of the *Poorna-Avatar,* while Anselm heard a thoroughly encouraging, but also challenging remark on his future work.

Then, on the veranda, one further and radiant smile from the shining face of the sun, as Sai Baba seems at this moment.

In the end, he even accepts a letter that we had carried to *Darshan* for quite a while.

Eventually, a shy and last *Padnamaskar,* the 'greeting and saluting of the feet' of a holy person, as a final and heart-felt Thank You! to Sathya Sai Baba.

Now that the interview was over, the atmosphere in the huge open-air *Sai Kulwant Hall* in front of the temple changed quickly. -
From still meditation to the hustle and bustle of all those many devotees.
Then we tried to answer the 'interested questions' from all around as politely and briefly as we could, while we were walking to our apartment already.

Finally we were grateful to be able to center ourselves again - and to share our thoughts and feelings about this loving and magic encounter with Sathya Sai Baba.

How often had we had long discussions, between the two of us and with some friends, in which the 'authentic nature' of Sai Baba's miracles was questioned.

Before, we had already personally seen several of his manifestations - mostly of *Vibhuti,* holy ash, but also of rings and pendants - but only during *Darshan,* in front of the temple, plus in some videos and films on Sai Baba.

Now, however, we had seen several manifestations in a row from close up - and with no tricks visible at all!
Quite the contrary:
Both of those rings that were created by Swami at the end of the interview fit on first try, and precisely on the finger that was indicated by him - which is not so easy without taking measurements beforehand, as any good goldsmith will affirm!

Or in other words, whoever or from where Sai Baba may have been - he has continuously demonstrated throughout his life that our scientific knowledge of today, which we sometimes are so 'proud of', is very limited indeed.

And he did so by transcending many laws of physics, chemistry and biology that are so far known to us - and that many times a day and day for day in his long life!

In this book, you have already found the reports on several awesome 'miracles' of Sai Baba that are far more impressive than what we have been allowed to see - and an abundance of them can be found in the literature and the media.
He was not only able to create jewellery - no!
Crystals and rosaries, cold liquids as well as hot food - all of these manifested from his divine hands.

But what, Dear Reader, do all these amazing 'miracles' - as they appear to our eyes - indicate?

A seemingly human being that is capable of turning rain on or off at will, who can create currency notes and airplane-tickets by a move of his hand - and who even can produce a 'vertical rainbow'* out in nature, as one of his visitors had challenged him to do.
*See: *Baskin, Diane: Divine Memories of Sathya Sai Baba*

And a person who can make a closed rose-bud bloom in a moment, just by touching it.

But when someone who saw this commented:
'Yes, Swami - you can do all these wonderful things, only we normal humans can't!'

Sai Baba replied: 'Oh yes, you can do that, too!' and then went on to tell that person to also touch one of the buds on that rose-bush.

And lo and behold: This bud bloomed to a full rose in no time as well . . .

As 'impossible' as these feats may appear to us, Sai Baba often used to refer to his constantly flowing 'miracles' only as his 'visiting cards'.

Calling cards that make sure we finally arrive at the understanding that his unassuming human form was inhabited by an infinite Divine Soul.

And the rest of our journey with Sai Baba 'was history', so to speak.

At the time of this inspiring and enormously motivating interview that Sathya Sai Baba had blessed us with, back then, in October 2000, we didn't know how long it would take us to make good on Anselm's optimistic promise:

'Swami, this is the beginning of a book!'
during this memorable exchange.

Next to lots of work at home in Munich, Germany, we were very grateful to return to *Prashanti Nilayam* in the years 2001-2002, also for divine and beautiful Christmas celebrations - with many angelic songs from a variety of religions!

But in the following years we were so busy with work, with taking care of our aging and dying parents - and with some health-issues of our own that we couldn't go to India.
Which meant a gap of seven long years without seeing Swami in person!

Those were difficult years, but we went to sing *Bhajans* with the Munich Sai Baba group whenever we could.

And we strengthened our connection to the *inner Swami* by doing Seva, by meditating and also by further reading and viewing the available books, newsletters and media by and on *Sri Sathya Sai Baba.*

All of this helped us a lot, when the time of letting go of our two remaining parents finally appeared.

In the middle of all the grief, confusion and new tasks that their 'shedding of their mortal coils' had caused - Anselm's mother in 2006, at 86 years and then still Gabriele's father in 2008, at almost 98 years - plus all the practice work, we weren't thinking of a journey to India any more.

But we had heard and seen in the media that Sai Baba's physical health seemed to have declined since he had an accident in 2003, when he was operated and had begun to make use of a mobile chair.
Therefore, we had started to make plans for a return to our beloved Swami in beautiful India for Christmas 2009 - and for New Year's celebrations 2010!

At the same time, we still remembered that Sai Baba had shown this pronounced interest in our manuscript at the beginning of the interview in 2000 - but we hadn't gotten around to expanding those pages into a book yet.

And this was a real predicament, as we clearly felt that we should have something 'book-like' along when we were returning to Swami now - nine full years after that unforgettable interview!

Therefore we started to compile a tome with the poems, texts and photographs we had collected, which mostly was done during the months before our flight to India.
And we even finished it on time!

Although this was a rather difficult journey to India and to *Prashanti Nilayam* in some ways - first road blocks, then lodging problems and sickness - we eventually were able to dissolve all of these by Baba's grace.
And we were ever so grateful to be in Sai's presence again. But there were so many, many people now. -
And no more interviews.

Saying goodbye to the Body

Also Sai Baba's outer appearance seemed very different now from his vigorous stance that we remembered from our last visit in 2002.
Despite that, he was still giving *Darshan,* while sitting in his mobile chair that was faithfully pushed by some of the students from the Sai University.

Besides the accident in 2003, which had made longer walking difficult, Sai Baba's body had suffered several minor strokes, causing a certain slackening of the left side of his face plus an impairment of speech, which mostly was an audible whisper by now, which often was amplified by a translator.
Facing all this, Sai Baba was as sharp and focused as ever in his dedicated service to the many and always further increasing visitors from India and around the globe.

At age 84, he was still 'on duty' for *Darshan* during most afternoons and even on some mornings.
Evidently, Sai's seemingly frail physical state had in no way diminished his transcendental powers, as we could see during *Darshan,* if only from a distance.
Baba was still manifesting holy ash, *Vibhuti,* and sometimes also a ring or pendant while giving Darshan.

And we even were able to bring our first 'prototype' of a book to *Darshan* in the beautiful *Sai Kulwant Hall* on one of these afternoon meetings!

Being in Sai Baba's aura again like this quickly recharged our 'spiritual batteries' and gave us new heart to go on with our writing process.
Already in the *Ashram* we began, by collecting ideas and discussing fitting themes for a book that would mostly be centered on healing psycho-somatic trauma and on ways to re-vitalize love and cooperation on all levels of our human relationships - in all the families and societies of this world.
And we continued with those preparations back home, along with the work in our practices.

At the same time, we still remembered our inspiring stay with Sai Baba only some months ago - and both of us were worried that his divine soul might be deciding to leave this service-worn and slowly faltering body, and possibly sooner than we all were hoping.
Therefore we decided to make one further journey to *Prashanti Nilayam* in the beginning of 2011.
Just some weeks before, Sai Baba had celebrated his 85th birthday with around half-a-million visitors.

And when we saw Swami again during *Darshan,* he still seemed somewhat frail - but he also was in full control of all interactions and functions, while giving help and advice to the ones around him as usual.
Now we were grateful to witness Swami's work and to bask in his divine aura again - and at the same time, we found the strong motivation to finally get going with our 'book to be'.

And so we sat in our room in the Ashram and wrote first drafts, whenever we had the time for it.

Anselm wrote by hand and Gabriele did the typing into a tiny lap-top we had brought with.

When our weeks at the Ashram ended, we felt spiritually recharged and centered again by our frequent nearness to Sathya Sai Baba - and we were especially grateful for the progress we had made with our texts.

By the time we were leaving the *Ashram*, somewhere in February 2011, Sai Baba was fully active in directing all the goings-on of the Ashram and of his manifold and awe-inspiring projects and institutions.

Hoping that Sai Baba, the all-powerful *Avatar* of our age, would soon heal those disturbing ailments of his body - as he had done on previous occasions, when his body had been seriously ill - we were now saying our inner *'Namaste'* in grateful spirits, when we set out for a short retreat of 'writing vacation' at the energizing shores of the Indian ocean.

This was a creative time that we enjoyed - but when we returned to Bangalore for our return flight to Germany, around the end of March 2011, we were shocked and sad to hear that our beloved Swami had been brought into his own super-specialty heart-clinic, and evidently because his heart-function was decreasing.

For weeks, all the millions of Sai devotees around the globe were praying fervently that Sai Baba would work one more of his amazing miracles to cure his body.
And he probably could have done that.
But he had other plans.
Sai Baba had given us a very gentle transition, as he had first reduced his physical presence for a while, and then by those weeks at the hospital, which prepared us at least somewhat in accepting Swami's final decision in this life, when he left his human body on
Easter Sunday, 24th of April 2011.

In those weeks and months after Swami's departure, we felt a bit like small children, whose parents had just left the planet.
And this sadness stayed with us, while we increased the focus on our inner Swami - and on some surprising and guiding *'Sai-Chronicities'* that occasionally showed us the way in our writings.
But then we remembered Sai Baba's: 'Do your duty!', his: 'Love all, serve all!' - and finally also his impish smile, together with that elating:
'Be happy!', which we had heard from him so directly.

Therefore, we picked ourselves up again - and life, work and writing continued in gratitude.
In the following years we returned to the main *Ashram* a couple of times for a deeper connection with Sai Baba's aura, to recharge our batteries and to find his inspiration for our slowly growing book.

Getting the Task done

After some quite adventurous events while travelling we were just about to generate time to continue and finish our writings in 2013, when obstacles appeared in form of some personal health issues.
When we had solved them as well as possible with the help of friendly and competent colleagues, we made a last minute decision to return to *Prashanti Nilayam,* the abode of peace supreme, in order to mend our rather wounded bodies and dejected spirits after the major operations we had had.

And sure enough, in Sai Baba's home we soon were able to replenish our parched souls - while we gained new zest to tackle our book for good now. And we promised to bring it to him at his grave, his *Mahasamadhi.*

Therefore we left Prashanti Nilayam writing, more or less - even while we were grateful for some sunny days of rest and relaxation at the shores of the Indian Ocean we continued working on the chapters of our text.
And for the next two years, 2014-2015, we applied every minute of our free time to this project.

By the end of 2015, we had produced an 'official book', with ISBN-number, that we had created - together with a small editing team - by desk-top publishing, which we later had printed at a local printing company.

And we brought the resulting tome in German language on a chip to Sai Baba's tomb in *Prashanti Nilayam,* with prayers for his blessings at his *Mahasamadhi*.

It contains some shorter introductory texts, but also longer novel-like chapters, which are all focussed on improving and healing individual trauma and dysfunctional behaviour, ailing relationships and families, and - finally - the overly aggressive and often militant attitude of our present human nations.

If you, Dear Reader, are interested in this path towards love and cooperation on the many levels of our human societies, you will find a short description and weblinks for our two English books:
The Pegasus-Paradise and *Alice - through Fire and Water* at the end of this book, which have - just as the book you are reading right now - evolved from the original German text.

Now you know the connection between Sathya Sai Baba, our life with him and the books we wrote in the process. It is our ongoing prayer to Swami that those books are somewhat resembling the ones he may have intended us to write.

As this has been clarified so far, we would like to return to some further memorable events in Sai Baba's life.

Swami's Teachings through his Miracles

Dear Readers, the following pages will give you some reminders of several episodes in Sai Baba's life. As with the other events we've mentioned earlier in this book, we are quoting from memory - for more detail, please see the sources in the bibliography.

As we are slowly approaching the end of this book now, we'd like to share some of the amazing incidents in Swami's exchange with the ones around him, while we're trying to fathom the possible meaning together.

Most Sai devotees know that Sai Baba's life was always resonating with divine and miraculous powers from the very beginning, like the musical instruments that began playing all by themselves at night when Swami's mother *Easwaramma* was pregnant with him.

Later on, small Sai - or *Bala Sai* - who at that time was still carrying his civil name *Sathya Narayena Raju,* often used to 'manifest' pens, erasers, pencils and stationary from his school-bag for his little friends, frequently along with sweets or fruit!

And at the same time - even as a child - Sathya taught his friends to sing sacred songs, *Bhajans,* plus to help the ones who needed it. -
And also to do their duty with a loving spirit.

A rare Transformation

Later on in school, young Sathya had to find out one day, that the other, more roughly disposed boys in his class used to collect frogs or toads in their free time - only to 'play' some rather unseemly 'games' with those poor animals.

Small Sathya didn't like this at all, as he despised the use of violence in any form.
But the other boys stayed stubborn and didn't care about Sathya's firm advice to leave those frogs alone.

Then Sai decided to teach them a lesson.
When they had collected a sizable basket with frogs and toads again, young Sathya quickly nabbed that basket and ran away with it.
When the other boys caught up with him, he just placed the whole thing upside-down on the ground!

And when the boys threatened him to return the frogs now immediately, or else . . .
He only lifted the basket for them.

But instead of frogs or toads, a whole swarm of pigeons was suddenly air-born from underneath that basket! -

A winging message in full flight for the other boys, who stood in utter disbelief around their divine classmate.

Solace in a Name

Next, we'd like to invite you to the well-known, central and life-changing scene in the youthful life of then fourteen years old Sathya.
While his mother and grandfather had mostly accepted his super-human nature already, according to the signs of his divinity he had shown them, Sathya's father and older brother were both rather sceptical.

On that special day, Sathya had returned home from school - only to throw his textbooks into the corner of the room, declaring that he wasn't the family's young Sathya any more, because he now was Sai Baba and his followers, his *devotees* needed him.

And when his father accosted him in no uncertain terms to reveal his true identity a while later, his son asked for a handful of fresh Jasmine flowers.
Having gotten those flowers, Sathya smiled gently at his somewhat unnerved father.
And while he was tossing the flowers to the ground in one sweeping movement, the youngster announced:
'I am Sai Baba!'
to his surprised and speechless family.

Because there, on the floor, the flowers had taken the form of exactly those letters in the local *Telugu* language that spelled just this, *Sai Baba*, Divine Mother and Divine Father in one person.

With this seemingly so simple gesture, Sathya Sai Baba was speaking to his family and to all of us in this world in several ways.

First of them was, of course, the declaration of his personal *Avatarhood* by saying - and flower-writing - 'Yes, I am Sai Baba, the reincarnation of that same Divine Soul as it was present in the holy man *Shirdi Sai Baba!'*

On a second plane, Sai Baba had provided direct proof for the claim of his own divinity - in form of that beatific 'writing on the ground' that spelled the advent of benevolent Divine Parents for the deeply sleeping humanity, and this in fragrant Jasmine flowers!

And thirdly, the global human species urgently needed this advent of love Divine on earth, as all nations were looking at a sinister 'writing on the wall' at that time -
it was the year 1939. - Where are we in March 2022?

But in the middle of the beginning of this horrible worldwide apocalypse, a youngster in British India confirmed, as it seemed, just by throwing those Jasmine flowers:

'All this madness will pass. What is going to remain is the divine love of this Avatar of Sai, which is as sweet as the scent of these Jasmine flowers!'

The following episode from young Sai Baba's life - also well documented - happened only a little while later.

Please let them live, Sir!

Again we quote from memory. Sai Baba was still in the middle of his teenage years, when a British official with his driver and jeep appeared in the area.
The man, who had a passion for hunting, had therefore brought his precision gun with to earn himself an especially 'worthy trophy' in the beautiful surroundings of Puttaparthi, Sai Baba's small home town.

And after some searching to and fro, the hunter finally sighted his dreams come true, which was a really huge and beautiful Bengal tiger!
Not given to thinking twice, he fired - and the tiger fell.

Next, the two men loaded the tiger's body onto the back of their jeep, to have it later made into a trophy by an expert taxidermist.
Now their drive went smoothly, until they had reached the vicinity of *Puttaparthi*, where the jeep gave one final grunt - and then refused to move any further.

The driver really did his best to persuade the recalcitrant engine to start again, but all measures proved futile.
The two men were about to get desperate, when the driver suddenly remembered about a young holy man in Puttaparthi that might be able to help them.

And even the sceptic western hunter was open to that in his predicament.

They met young Sai in the street and asked for his help. At this, he went with them to their jeep. When he had seen the dead tiger on that car, he told them directly:
'Sir, you just have killed that tiger, who was the mother of three cubs.
Please let them live, Sir!

First go back and find them.
They are too small still to fend for themselves - and they urgently need their own mother's milk, or at least a suitable substitute to survive.
Therefore kindly bring them to a zoo, where they can be taken care of.
And one more thing.
Are you really sure that hunting makes you happy?
Take your time with an answer - and perhaps from now on go 'hunting' with your *camera* instead!
Oh, by the way, your jeep is fine now.
So you can go and pick up those three tiger babies!'

When Sai Baba had admonished the amazed British hunter in comparable words, the white man felt rather ashamed by the all-knowing divine soul in the young Indian Guru who stood in front of him.
They quickly said good-bye - and then rushed back with their jeep to find the cubs.
Surprisingly, it had started on first try - as if there had never been any problem at all!

Also Baba's next prediction proved true.

Near the place of their encounter with the mother, they found the three wailing and hungry cubs!

Then the British man made good on Swami's advice and brought those cubs to a zoo, where they had a future.

But the story doesn't end there, as most Sai devotees know from related pictures.
The - hopefully - ex-hunter had realized that this killing of animals still remained killing - and that he didn't really want his formerly so desired tiger-trophy any longer.

Therefore - and after preparation - he brought the tiger skin plus head to Sai Baba as a present.

And Sai Baba didn't only accept it - but later on, he even placed his chair in the *Mandir* or temple on it.
Where he often sat during *Bhajans* and *Meditation* - and that for many decades.

'Transform the killing hunter in you!'
is a possible message that might be emanating from that tiger skin and its head.

This awe-inspiring tiger-episode from young Sai Baba's life leaves us with numerous big question marks.

How did the divine director unfold this play to begin with? So that jeep 'broke down' at the 'proper place', in order to make a meeting with Swami possible?

And how could Sai not only know the whole tragedy of the tiger-mom - but also the imminent fate of the three abandoned tiger-cubs?!
And eventually, who had given the broken jeep a new life - out there, in the middle of nowhere - so it could be started on first try?

Even though some may call this coincidence or trickery - we have found another conclusion for these seemingly magic events.
Sai Baba has often explained that they are just aspects of his nature - and what we are usually calling 'miracles' is happening due to his divine *Sankalpa,* his instantly realizing infinite will-power.
Which, as it seems to us, directs not only all those games and plays, small and large, here on our tiny planet earth - but maybe even far beyond . . .

Spotless Devotion

From the tiger incident with all the connected questions we move on now in Sai Baba's life for about one and a half decades.

For several years, he had received his many visitors in the *Old Mandir,* the 'Old Temple', as it was later called.

But Swami's divine love, including healings and amazing miracles, had brought ever increasing waves of many new Sai devotees to sleepy *Puttaparthi* town.

And Sai Baba, who was going to turn 25 years* old in 1950, needed a new and bigger temple to accommodate the growing crowds - and adequate living quarters for Swami as well.

*In Indian counting, a person is already one year old at the time of birth.

For this purpose, land had been purchased before with the support of donations by wealthy devotees and by way of non-profit trusts.

This land was going to house Sai Baba's future Ashram, *Prashanti Nilayam,* the abode of peace supreme, in the years to be - but the construction of the *New Mandir,* Swami's new and permanent temple, was in full swing already at the end of the 1940s.

For Puttaparthi standards of those days, the large new temple building seemed 'way too big', according to some 'experts' and critics.
But Sai Baba knew what he was doing - and even told those critics that more and larger buildings were going to follow, for the benefit of his devotees.
Including an airport for large airplanes in later years!

Hardly anybody could imagine that in the end of the 1940s . . . But the building of the *New Mandir,* the heart of Swami's future Ashram, was nearly finished.
Its first stage was inaugurated in 1950.

Later, in the beginning of the 1970s, it was transformed into a larger temple, with three new domes on the roof.

In order to complete the oriental domes, situated on top of the ellipsoid two-storied structure, many steel-tubes had to be welded together to later support the bricks and concrete of the domes.
This is the next scene from Sai Baba's life that we'd like to remember together with you, Dear Reader.
The just mentioned welding of those tubes on top of the temple was still going on late at night to finish the work on time.
All the welders were rather dirty and also covered with welding-grease. The air was filled with a din of sounds from sawing, hammering and welding the steel, mixed with wisps of smoke from the metal-melting flame in this work-filled and torch-lit night.

But suddenly a youthful Sai Baba appeared with a small entourage - right there, in the middle of those sweating and welding men - and in the middle of the night!
Why did he do that?

Because he was happy with the discipline and devotion of those metal workers - who were doing their hard job way beyond their regular hours into the night, while happily singing *Bhajans*.

And now this - some of the welders lost all restraint in their spiritual fervor, as they fell at Swami's feet, while touching them and his robe with their dirty hands.

Which left traces on the cloth that were clearly visible, even despite the nighttime setting.

And all of Sai Baba's companions knew, how important good hygiene and proper appearance were to him.
Therefore one of them shouted:
'Spots, Swami!' pointing at Sai Baba's robe.

But to everyone's surprise, Swami only chuckled and replied something like:
'No, no! - Those are just flowing tears of joy, because of their spotless devotion!'

What a gentle and equal-minded remark from this divine being to his material helpers.

Be flexible and let go of too much etiquette or even harshness, when the situation rather evokes empathy instead - might be a possible conclusion for us to learn from this early and simple but also charming and thought-provoking incident.

The construction of the enlarged *New Mandir* was now completed successfully, so it could finally be inaugurated in 1974.

During the 1990s, the huge *Sai Kulwant* hall was added in front of the Mandir, to provide shade and shelter for the many devotees.

From this heart-felt exchange between Sathya Sai Baba and his welding crew, we move on now to recollect the specifics of one further scene situated in one of the earlier decades of Swami's life.

Healing in the Jungle

Sai Baba was on a road trip with a group of devotees. They had stopped near the looming trees of a natural jungle area and left their cars to take a walk amongst those silent sentinels of this jungle-like forest.

Swami and one of his devotees were absorbed in a lively conversation, while the others had gone ahead already.

And exactly in this moment, with only this one devotee near him - Swami felt a sharp sting in his foot!

Both men looked at the cause immediately and saw a lethal viper disappear in the undergrowth!

What a difficult turn of events.
Because Sai Baba had explained many times, what he always documented by his own behaviour and actions, which is that he used his super-human powers only for the benefit of others!

But now this untoward snakebite jeopardized Sai Baba's whole further Avatarhood.

Then the devotee, who was with Swami in this crucial moment, felt helpless and desperate, as he watched the body of his beloved master shaking dangerously from the rapid effects of that life-threatening venom.

But what was that?! With a painfully distorted face and perspiring heavily, Sai Baba gave that man a shaky nod, while he barely managed to lift his 'magic hand' a little - but nothing happened!

Then Swami pointed at his companion - and then was just about to collapse.

Finally the devotee understood the message that Swami was faintly conveying.

And he started to imitate the circular movement of the right hand, as he had seen it so often when Sai Baba had manifested *Vibhuti,* sacred ash, or other objects for his devotees.

Somewhat shy and incredulous at first -
'This is working perfectly with Swami, who is God - but how can it ever with a simple human being like me?!' -
the man soon circled his hand as best as he could, while he saw how Swami's body was shaking and swaying from the lethal venom.

Later on, the devotee reported that he suddenly felt, how something was pushing its way through the middle of his palm, when he did this circular movement.

According to Sai Baba's gestures, he then grabbed that object - and when he looked at his hand, he found a small pendant on a string, to be worn around the neck.

Now the man finally realized what he had to do!
While Swami's body was just about to fall, that faithful devotee took the manifested pendant - and hung it right around Sai Baba's neck.

And from one moment to the next, his severe symptoms from the snakebite disappeared - and he could breathe normally again.
Then Swami thanked the devotee - and continued on the path, while throwing the pendant into the woods!

Because the healing had happened by now, it wasn't needed any longer. A memorable event in Swami's life, with some special twists - for the benefit of the whole human family.
Source: *Ganapati, Ra: Baba: Sathya Sai, Tome I and II.*

And there is one further situation from Sai Baba's life that we would like to remember with you, Dear Reader, which is focussing on some really far-reaching aspects of his divine nature.

The setting of these events was the India of the 1970s or '80s, and we again quote from memory, as well as we can remember.

The safe Instrument

This story begins with a well-placed Indian official, who was working for a major corporation during those years. This person lived in a city hundreds of kilometres away from Puttaparthi town, and with that, also from Swami's Ashram *Prashanti Nilayam*.

Now this official had met with some tough difficulties in his private life and at work - quite an extended streak of 'very bad luck'.

And some more than harsh words from his superior had given him the rest.

After work, he had returned home in a state of inner turmoil and depression.

And as nothing seemed to make good sense to him any longer, he eventually brought out a hand-gun he owned and began loading it.
Then he lifted the weapon to end his cumbersome life.

At the same time, but in that seemingly far away place, *Prashanti Nilayam,* abode of peace supreme, Sai Baba was surrounded by a group of devotees.

In the middle of a sentence, he suddenly exclaimed:
'Don't shoot!'
while he fell into a motionless trance-state.

The ones around him were familiar with this already, as they had witnessed before how Swami was leaving his body in this state, in order to go travel and work on the inner plane.

Back to that desperate official, who is just about to point the gun at himself, hoping to terminate his so bleak-felt worldly existence.

But in this moment of maximum tension in his life -
there is a loud knock at the entrance door of the house.
Dismayed, the man puts down the weapon - trying to think of a quick hiding-place for it, so he can go and see who is at the door.

Eventually he ran to the bedroom and put the gun under a pillow.
Then he went to open the door.

There he was greeted by tree people unknown to him - but who skillfully managed to involve him into an extended discussion on a variety of subjects that were somehow related to himself.

And when he finally said good-bye to them to go back into the house, he felt a trace of new faith in his heart.

Until he suddenly remembered the hidden gun!
So he ran to the bedroom and lifted the pillow - but there was no weapon any more!

While Sai Baba now woke up from his deep trance in *Prashanti Nilayam* and told the circle of devotees around him all the details of this incident, also from the perspective of the three unknown visitors.

Then he showed them the loaded gun, which he had also 'brought with'.

As it was clear now that the official would be severely worried about his missing weapon, the circle around Swami proposed to send a telegram immediately to that man by wire.
The text was to indicate that the gun was safe now.
But then there were some second thoughts about using the word 'weapon' or 'gun' in such an official telegram - and who might read it.

In the end, a compromise was found and the telegram read about like this:
'The instrument is safe with me.'
Sathya Sai Baba

If many or most of you, Dear Readers, can only shake your head in disbelief or laugh out loud at these reports of Sai Baba's super-human powers - we understand you quite well, as we also had our doubts in the beginning.
The reason for this is that beings of genuine divinity with their far-reaching powers have visited the earth only many hundreds or even millennia of years apart - and therefore we are not so very familiar with them.

But this has all changed with Sathya Sai Baba's advent, who certainly was the most accessible and also the best documented God-Person in human history.

And it is the main intention of this book to remember his awe-inspiring life and work, based on the experiences of the authors with Sai Baba during their journeys to his *Ashram* in India, and founded on their continuous study of the Sai media since 1984.

Therefore we hope that this bright rainbow of different incidents from Sathya Sai Baba's life and from our own encounters with him that we have put together in this book will be a first incentive for you, Dear Readers, to start your own quest into the infinite and infinitely beautiful realms of the triple Avatar Sai Baba!

Before you do that, however, there is one final situation from Sai Baba's life that we would like you to remember together with you.

It depicts a special group situation, which gave a rare insight on the way Sathya Sai Baba himself might have perceived the world.

Can you let me see it?

This situation has been documented in the national and international Sai media in recent years.
Here the summary of the events, quoted from memory.

In this group present with Sai Baba at that time, there was a well known physician from the USA, *Dr. Michael Goldstein*, who had been active in leading the US and also the International Sai Organisation for years, on which Swami had made some very positive comments.

All of a sudden, Dr. Goldstein dared to ask Sai Baba a special question:
'Swami, how do we and the world look to you?
Probably different from our perception.
Can you let me see it?
If this is permissible to ask, Swami?'

But Sai Baba fulfils our wishes only, when this helps us along in our life.

In a gentle voice, mother Sai answered Dr. Goldstein:

'Oh no, Goldstein!
If I let you see my inner realm, you will not want your body, your wife or your work any longer - and would that really be good?
Continue your projects, they help!'

About like this was Swami's friendly reply to Dr. Michael Goldstein's intrepid question.
But why is this simple exchange important enough to us to place it at the very end of this book?

Because it illuminates an essential aspect in Sai Baba's divine personality so directly.
This is the quality of the original source of love in its eternal light and infinite fullness, in which Sai Baba was constantly at home - with an intensity that often went far beyond the scope and stability of any of us humans.
And he has told us so quite often.
But Dr. Goldstein's brave question resulted in that divine twist towards direct inner experience -
setting us all searching for our *CIA*, our
Constant Integrated Awareness.

But why should we be interested in this odd but somehow familiar acronym at all?
CIA - Constant Integrated Awareness -
what does it mean to us?
Sathya Sai Baba has coined this abbreviation *'CIA'* in that special sense - and he is also the living answer to those questions.
Because all of us have a profound yearning - consciently or unconsciently - for this *CIA-state* of deep inner peace, where our engagement in our worldly and time-bound tasks is at the same time constantly integrated with the awareness of our real self, which is the eternal light of divinity, right in the middle of our heart.

And Sai Baba has invited us to find out which path leads us to this inner place we all are longing for.

Is it money, land or power?

Maybe to some degree, if used wisely. But there is no peace or inner light inherent in those material things.

'My life is my message!' was Swami's frequent motto by which he taught us through his personal example, how this *Constant Integrated Awareness or CIA* can be found - and permanently kindled anew in our life.

Seva and *Sadhana,* loving service to others and personal meditation on the infinite light within us, are the safety fences on that road.

And Sai Baba gave us two main guiding messages for our journey through life, which are:

'Love All, Serve All!'
and
'Help Ever, Hurt Never!'
by his own divine life and as hallmarks for the whole range of his educational, health related and other social projects.

Sathya Sai Baba was the incarnation of the
True Divine Parents of Humanity
free to access, see and experience for everybody.

And Swami dared to remind us - in an engaged and global approach - of some themes that are not so very popular in our 'modern material world'.

These themes are equivalent to the central insight that the values truth, righteousness, non-violence and love are the indispensable prerequisites, if we want to achieve inner and outer peace - or even the divine bliss of eternity in our heart.
Sathya, Dharma, Ahimsa, Prema, Shanti and *Ananda* - Sathya Sai Baba has instructed humanity for decades along those lines, by his daily tireless work and by his astounding divine legacy.

And this at a crucial time in human history that needs to listen to the message of the *Avatar* more urgently than ever before - in order to then take action in an inspired and energetic way.
Action to save the planet as well as all of humanity from the destructive ego in us.

Sai Baba has given humankind a gentle but giant shove in that direction, as only can be done by a God Person.
And we as humans can contribute to this collective shift in our personal and global awareness and behaviour, everybody according to their abilities.

But the very minimum we can do in return for Sai Baba's divine life and work is to be happy and to be grateful.

Epilogue

Dear Readers,
of course there are uncounted fascinating episodes from Sathya Sai Baba's life that we weren't able to mention in this brief panoramic introduction to the person and work of the Avatar of our age.

But for now, let's be content with one last question.
A question that may also have appeared in your mind at times while reading those reports in this book.
And this question asks:

'Where did the phenomenon Sai Baba originate?'

Swami himself has at least indicated occasionally that he is from 'somewhere else', by saying something like:
'If all of you only knew where I'm really from . . . !'

And there is a minimum of two well-documented further telltale incidents from his life that might be able to shed some additional light on this unfathomable question.

The first one is situated right at the beginning of Swami's embodied existence in this incarnation.

His mother *Easwaramma* reported those events, as they had happened to her, when she still was rather early in her pregnancy with him.

She repeatedly answered questions related to this by recalling how she had gone out of the house back then to get water from the well, while she was feeling a quiet inner happiness about her beginning pregnancy.

Then, when she was just standing there, near the well, she looked up and suddenly saw a sphere of light that was fast rolling towards her, way too quickly to evade.
Now that light reached her and merged with her, which caused her to faint for a moment.

But soon, when she awoke again - helped by her mother in law, who had found her - she didn't notice anything unusual, except perhaps for some peaceful and elated feelings that surprised her.

When *Easwaramma* later told those events to others, while Sai Baba was present himself, he sometimes used to comment in words like:

'Do you hear what she is saying?
This was no normal birth! It was an *Advent.*'

At the same time, Sai Baba always honoured his parents.
But he also clearly denoted that he didn't experience them as 'his' parents - much rather, he called them:
'The parents of this body' while indicating himself.
And sometimes he lovingly called them 'the girl in the house' or 'the boy in the house', when he had declared his Avatarhood.

Also in Swami's years as a young boy he was steeped in his God-awareness already, which sometimes caused unusual exchanges with the family.

For instance, when his mother *Easwaramma* entered the room and the little boy Sathya went on to comment something like:

'Oh look! *Maya* has appeared again!'

Understandably, the mother was somewhat surprised at this, as *'Maya'* means nothing else than *'Illusion'* in the ancient Indian language of the *Vedas, Sanskrit.*

But soon she had learnt to understand that her 'small Sathya' was living on the plane of Divinity itself in his heart - a plane, where all transient, material phenomena are mainly experienced as passing illusions.

Advaita
Non-Duality

God is none and God is all,
God is great and God is small;
Fairy-wing and tiger tall:
God is none and God is all.

Timeless Time

With this we are now reaching the second situation that might help clarify Sai Baba's whereabouts a bit - if in a somewhat paradoxical way.

Again we quote from memory, according to the national and international Sai media.

If we recollect correctly, the setting of those events was *Trajee Brindavan,* Sai Baba's home in his *Ashram* located at *Brindavan,* near Whitefield, a suburb of Bangalore, today *Bengaluru.*

At that time, in the beginning of the 1990s, Swami had a visitor in his house in Brindavan, whom we know from the beginning of this book already.

His name is *Keith Critchlow;* a UK architect specialized in sacral architecture. Remember him?

He is the architect of Sai Baba's amazing marvel of a Healing Temple, the huge Super-Specialty Hospital and heart clinic near *Puttaparthi.*

Sai Baba had once invited him to his home in Brindavan, where Mr. Critchlow experienced the following, as he has later communicated and published.
Therefore, we only summarize the events.

Sitting there, in one of the rooms of Swami's beautiful house, Mr. Critchlow suddenly noticed that there were *two cuckoo-clocks* on one of the walls.
Therefore he asked:
'Swami, do you like cuckoo-clocks?'
And Sai Baba seems to have answered
in his inimitable way:
'I don't need time - I am time!'
as a revelation to Mr. Critchlow and to all of us.

And now we must resist the temptation to interpret those events in Sai Baba's life in terms of his original home and living quarters in this cosmos - or beyond?
What remains instead, however, is the divine message and giant legacy from two incarnations of the *Sai Avatar*, *Shirdi Sai Baba* and *Sathya Sai Baba*, which is the best inheritance our so far strife-ridden humanity could have hoped for.

Finally it remains to us, to hope and pray with all our heart that the *'Third Man'* of the Sai Avatar
Prema Sai Baba
will show himself according to Sathya Sai Baba's own prediction in due time to guide humanity further away from outdated aggressions, war and self-destruction and instead towards the *Golden Age* of peace, prosperity and cooperation.
And everybody can help with this project Golden Age for humankind.

Om Sai Ram

The Authors

Gabriele Breucha has a Diploma as an Oecotrophologist Dipl. Oec. troph. or Nutritional Scientist and is a licensed Healing Practitioner and Psychotherapist with her own practice in Munich.
Further, she is a consultant on Bio-identical Hormones and an expert in both Eastern and Western Astrology, in Phytotherapy and in Homeopathy.

Anselm Keussen, Dr. med. / MD is a General Practioner, specialized in Depth-Psychology based Psychotherapy and is licensed as a Medical Psychotherapist, working in his practice in Munich, Germany.

When he had finished his university training in medical sciences - at LMU Munich plus one year of 4th year electives at St. Louis University Medical School, in neurology, neurophysiology lab and neonatal intensive care unit - he joined the COLOMAN therapy center - out in nature near Wasserburg and in Munich - as a medical psychotherapist (1981).

While studying in St. Louis, he also met his first wife, Nancy. She was the one, who found Howard Murphet's book: *'Sai Baba - Man of Miracles'* in an antiquarian bookshop. Later they had a daughter together, Sathya, who is married and a mother herself by now, while she is working as a teacher and manager.

The COLOMAN therapy center in southern Bavaria was smaller than the Californian Esalen institute, but in some ways also similar to it.
In the beginning, Janov's Primal Therapy plus Encounter Groups were frequently applied.
Only to be followed by Rebirthing, Gestalt, Transactional Analysis = TA and Core-/ Bioenergetics as well as Rolfing, Postural Integration and various forms of Gentle Body-Work and Massage.

Later on, Hakomi®, video-assisted work and the more systemic, or rather hypno-systemic approaches of Milton Erickson's work, Family Therapy work, NLP® and also Bert Hellinger's Systemic Family Constellations were employed there as well.

Besides, a host of spiritual programmes and groups were going on, from Christian Meditation practices to ZEN and Shamanism, with dancing, drumming and sweat-lodges, and including work with a Samadhi tank as well.

Dr. Anselm Keussen was working there from 1981-1994. During this time, he also wrote his dissertation on:

The Meta-Model of Psychoanalysis
An actualisation of Freud's ´Project of a Psychology for Neurologists´ from the perspective of modern neuro-physiology, psychology, and clinical psychotherapy
(1984).

Later, he trained and specialized in Depth-Psychology based Psychotherapy and started his own practice as a licensed Medical Psychotherapist (1991).

In 1985 Anselm - and since 1992 both of us - got in contact with *Sathya Sai Baba* of India, who deeply inspired, impressed and guided us - not only during several stays at his main Ashrams in Puttaparthi and Brindavan, but also in our night-to-night, day-to-day life. Although he seems to be physically 'absent' since 2011, we still continue to feel Sai Baba's loving and healing presence in many ways.

From 1990-1994 **Gabriele und Anselm** were working at the COLOMAN institute as a couple, married since 1992, seeing patients, couples and families, as well as leading groups, as they are also doing now in their individual practices and together.

Each eye

Each I
is Sai.

Websites on Sathya Sai Baba

https://www.sathyasai.org

http://www.saibaba.ws

http://saibaba.ws/miracles.htm

https://saisarathi.com

Further Books by the Authors

Website one:
www.alicetoday.eu
with *Reading Samples* from our Book:
Alice - through Fire and Water
Or: Where is Wonderland?
ISBN: 978-3-7528-4982-0

Website two:
www.the-pegasus-paradise.net
with *Reading Samples* from our Book:
The Pegasus-Paradise
Genesis 3.0
ISBN: 978-3-7543-9139-6

Selected Bibliography
Books on Spiritual Living

Anand, Deepak: Love Smile Now
An MBA Professor on Sathya Sai Baba

Barks & Green: The Illuminated Rumi

Baskin, D.: Divine Memories of Sathya Sai Baba

Castaneda, C.: The Eagle's Gift;
The Fire from within; The Power of Silence

Confucius: Analects

Daskalos/ Stylianos Atteshlis:
The Esoteric Teachings

Dora, H. J.: Glorious Moments with God - A Police Superintendent of India on Sathya Sai Baba

Field, R.: The Alchemy of the Heart

Galeone, P.: Padre Pio - My Father

Ganapati, R.: Baba: Sathya Sai - Tome 1 & 2

Griffiths, B.: The Marriage of East and West

***Footnote Family Life** p 12: This story was seen in various media, first was a talk by **Bert Hellinger** in the 1980s in Munich, Germany.*

Gokak, V.: Sai Baba: The Man and the Avatar

Hemadpant: Shri Sai Satcharita; on Shirdi Sai Baba

House, A.: Francis of Assisi

Kasturi, N.: Sathyam Sivam Sundaram - Tome 1-4
Biography of Sathya Sai Baba until 1979;
Loving God - An autobiography of Prof. N. Kasturi,
mainly depicting his life with Sathya Sai Baba

Krishnamurthi, J.: Talks in India 1948-1950 - in French:
De la Connaissance de Soi

Krystal, P.: Cutting the Ties that bind; Monkey Mind

Lao-Tzu: Tao Te Ching

Levin, H.: Heart to Heart; Good Chances - Meetings with
Sathya Sai Baba

Markides, K.: The Magus of Strovolos - see *Daskalos*

Mazzoleni, M.: A Catholic Priest meets Sai Baba

Mittelsten-Scheid, D.: In the Mirror of Silence

Murthy, B.N. Narasimha: Sathyam Sivam Sundaram
Sathya Sai Baba's Biography 1980-2001; Tome 5-7

Murphet, H.: Sai Baba: Man of Miracles

Sai Baba, S.: Sadhana; The Lamp of Love;
Upanishad Vahini; Prema Vahini

Sandweiss, S. H.: Sai Baba
The Holy Man and the Psychiatrist

Shankaracharya, A.: Tattva Bodha -
The Knowledge of Truth; Viveka Chudamani -
The Crest Jewel of Discrimination

Steindl-Rast, D.: A Listening Heart

Tagore, R.: Fireflies - Poems

Werfel, F.: Star of the Unborn

Wilber, K.: Grace and Grit; One Taste

Yogananda, P.: Autobiography of a Yogi

Yukteswar G.: The Holy Science

Advaita
Non-Duality

Love is none and Love is all,
Love is great and Love is small;
Fairy-wing and tiger tall:
Love is none and Love is all.

Om

Shanti

Shanti

Shanti